Jill and the Wild Horses

by Jemma Spark

Book Eleven of Jemma Spark's Jill Series

Epona Publishing

www.ponybookuniverse.com

Trade paperback ISBN 978-1-7637917-1-8

Jill Books

Jill Rides Cross Country (Jill Series Book 1)

Jill Has Two Horses (Jill Series Book 2)

Jill Goes Pony Trekking (Jill Series Book 3)

Jill and the Mystery of the Missing Horse (Jill Short Story)

Jill and the Steeplechaser (Jill Series Book 4)

Jill Dreams of a Dressage Horse (Jill Series Book 5)

Jill and the Horsemasters (Jill Series Book 6)

All Change at Blainstock Stables (Jill Series Book 7)

Jill's Ponies: Black Boy and Rapide (Jill Series Book 8)

The Adventures of Jill's Ponies (Jill Series Book 9)

Jill and the Prize Winners (Jill Series Book 10

The Jill Crewe Miscellany No. One (compendium and short stories)

Jill and the Wild Horses (Jill Series Book 11)

Table of Contents

Prologue

I feel I should explain the non-chronological order of this book in terms of the Jill series. I returned from Australia and leapt into the saga of *Jill and the Prize Winners* which is book 10. I didn't feel up to telling my beloved readers and the world at large about what happened in Australia. I had rather let the cat out of the bag in Book 9, *The Adventure of Jill's Ponies,* with the cataclysmic announcement that my father was not dead, but in fact alive and living in Australia. I just couldn't quite face up to telling you every detail. Now I have girded my loins and here it is, the 'Australian Adventure', which is technically Book 11. I have now started work on the book provisionally called, *Summer at Blainstock Stables,* which will be Book 12 and will pick up where *Jill and the Prize Winners* finished, and will also make reference to the two short stories in *Jill Crewe's Miscellany No. One.*

Chapter One – Going to Australia

I climbed the steps to the plane in mid-winter. There was a tingling dawn frost lit up by a dazzling low sun. Everything was crystal clear, and I had a pang of regret. For a moment I wanted to stay in Britain, my native land and not face the heat and dust of the Antipodes and meet a man who was my long-lost father, who I had believed was dead. Throughout my childhood, I nurtured vague, cherished, and well-polished memories of him since I was a tot. Now, all these easy illusions, more imaginings than anything else, were to be blown apart by the reality of him being a flesh and blood convicted murderer, rather than an angelic presence.

"There is something I have to discuss with you, Jill," said Mummy some days before I was due to leave for Australia.

I expected a litany of do's and don'ts, although, to be fair, this was not Mummy's usual style. I'm not sure why I expected her to suddenly become an instructor of correct behaviour at my advanced age of twenty years. Perhaps she was about to issue a note of caution about how to behave with the Heywards, the Australian family who had invited me to travel with them on a summer showjumping trip.

"This is a huge thing, and I'm afraid you may resent the fact that I haven't told you before. In truth, I've been turning it over in my mind for some time now."

I was barely listening, thinking about whether I had packed sufficient pairs of socks and underwear. Then, I contemplated the type of horses I was to showjump in a foreign land of dusty plains and sun-drenched bushland.

She persisted in her speech, which she must have rehearsed many times before this delivery. "Especially when I married Richard. I thought then that it might be something that I should do. But on balance, I decided that moving to Scotland with a new stepfather would be enough of a change for you to adjust to."

"Mummy, this is weird. What on earth are you going on about?" I asked impatiently, thinking that I wanted to go down to the stables and spend some time with my horses before I swanned off for weeks and weeks of what was essentially a holiday, leaving behind Linda, Hugh and John to do all the work at Blainstock Stables, our joint business venture.

"Jill, please just concentrate; sometimes you have the attention span of a gnat. This is *very, very* important."

It suddenly occurred to me that she was about to say that she was having another baby. Hamish was now a very naughty toddler, but surely, Mummy was getting a bit long in the tooth to have another child.

"Are you pregnant *again*?" I asked with just a hint of accusation.

"This is serious," she said impatiently.

"And another baby isn't?" I snapped churlishly.

"No, not at all, but this is *very* important. I must warn you that what I'm about to tell you is very serious. You must prepare yourself for a serious shock."

"Well, *tell me!*" I demanded. The words of warning were wheeling and turning in my mind like gulls above a spawning tide. My mother paused as if to gather her courage, and then the words came out.

"It's about your father."

Now, this floored me. When I was young my father had gone away on a business trip and never returned. He had died. I didn't even remember him very well. I suppose Mummy had quietly mourned him, but we had got on with our lives and moved from Wales to Pool Cottage in Chatton and managed very well on our own.

"He's not dead. He's alive."

There was a moment of ringing silence. I wondered if Mummy was going a bit batty. My father had been dead for years, dead as a doornail. However, as Charles Dickens had written, why is a doornail dead?

"I told you he was dead. I told everyone he was dead. But he wasn't."

"Why on earth would you do that?" I asked impatiently, not really believing her. At least not believing the bit about him not being dead, not the bit about telling everyone he was dead.

"Because he went to prison. He went to prison for a very long time. I suppose I couldn't bear the shame of it. I didn't want you growing up and people pointing at you and saying, 'There goes the murderer's daughter."

"My father was a murderer," I whispered in horror—finally, the shock of this news breaking through my careless disbelief.

"Well, he did kill someone, but it was an accident. No one but me believed him. They said it was deliberate, and he went to prison for a very long time. But he got out last year, and he's gone to Australia to make a new life for himself. I received a letter from him last week," she said.

"How did he know where to write to you?" I asked inconsequentially.

"We hadn't been corresponding for all those years. We thought it best to make a clean break of it. To give me and you a chance of a better life. But

when we moved up here, I wrote to the prison informing them of my change of address. Just in case."

"Oh!" was all I could manage to squeak.

"Who .. was killed?" I asked. I couldn't quite bring myself to say, 'Who did he kill?'

"It was his business partner. Your father went away. You know his name was David, and he found out that Jerry, his partner, had done something dastardly. When your father came back to England he had it out with him, and it came down to some pushing and shoving, and Jerry fell over, hit his head and died. It looked so suspicious, and they decided that your father had whacked him across the head deliberately."

"Gosh!" I gasped, feeling as if all the air was being sucked out of my lungs. "That sounds like something out of a penny dreadful."

"His parents, who lived in Wales, died while he was in prison. I think, in a way, they died of shame. Everyone in the village knew what had happened. That was one reason why we left Wales to go to Oxfordshire for a new start. He inherited their terraced house and it was sold. He wrote and wanted me to have the proceeds of the sale, but I explained that we were getting on very well now. That was before Richard lost all his money," she said a little ruefully. "I suggested he take the money and use it to set himself up with a new life."

"I suppose Australia is where we sent our convicts," I quipped, with a weak attempt at humour.

"Now that the Heywards have invited you, it might be an opportunity for you to meet him."

Again, there was one of those silences. I was finding it hard to process all this startling information. My father was alive! I suppose I had never really thought much about him. He had been a shadowy figure in my childish imagination. There were a couple of photos, grainy snapshots of him holding me as a baby, and one professional photo of Mummy's wedding. He had been tall and thin with blonde hair. I suppose that was where I got my blonde hair, as Mummy's had always been light brown. As they say in books, he had not been classically handsome but had a very pleasant countenance. I was still thinking of him in the past tense. It had indeed not occurred to me as a child that there was something malevolent in his face. I was thankful that the death of his partner had been an accident. Without even considering it, I believed that he was innocent of evil intent. He had been outraged by the corrupt practices of his partner and had been flailing about in the throes of righteous indignation.

You might wonder if I resented the fact that Mummy had kept this from me for all these years, if I felt betrayed by lies. But I didn't. I could see the impeccable reasoning behind her actions. I had never really felt the loss of a father, as I could barely remember ever having one. My best friend Ann had a father who was a remote figure who disappeared behind a newspaper at breakfast and caught the train to London every day. I supposed it was better to have a dead father than to live with the awful secret knowledge of being the progeny of a convicted murderer. That would have been a heavy weight upon my soul.

"I've wondered of late if that was one of the reasons why you haven't got yourself a boyfriend," said Mummy. She made it sound like I had gone shopping and forgotten to purchase myself a young man. I had been concentrating on gloves and handbags rather than a life companion. "You know, with Ann and Henry, and even Susan Pyke married to that man, Bartholomew. They grew up with fathers, and that prepared them for the idea of marriage."

Now, this did make me feel uncomfortable. Inside, I was twisting around in excruciating embarrassment. It sounded like Mummy was saying in some ineffable way that I was immature, unfit to grow into adulthood. I remembered my unfortunate infatuation with the dastardly Jack Lasky when I had gone to Porlock Vale. I was glad I had never mentioned that to Mummy. He had been forty years old but a very glamorous and attractive forty years old. Undoubtedly, someone might have diagnosed me as suffering from a complex whereby I was looking for a father. This was entirely untrue. It was simply a schoolgirl crush, and I had gotten over it!

I could have gone off on a tangent, hating this somewhat unfavourable examination of my psyche and obviously (!) deficient personality, but there was no time for such gruesome thoughts. I had to grapple with the fact of a father. Not just some shadowy figure who I had always fondly believed 'had had a way with horses' but a real live human being with a beating heart and a very unfortunate life story. He lived in Australia, and I was about to board an aeroplane and fly halfway around the world to find him.

"I know it's a big thing for you to cope with, and I would have preferred to have told you before. It was just the coincidence of Australia, with the chance that you might take the opportunity to meet him. I *had* to tell you. Have I done the right thing?" she looked at me searchingly. There was a note of pleading in her eyes. "Perhaps I should have told you a long time ago, but it was such a can of worms that I couldn't bring myself to do it".

"Can of worms," I echoed. It was a great big barrel of worms. Then, my imagination began to zoom into the most over-used of all tropes. "Next, you'll be telling me I have a twin brother – called Bill! Bill and Jill! He's living

in Wales, brought up by my grandparents, and when they died, he went to the local orphanage," I continued constructing a Victorian melodrama. Reflecting on this delusion later I realised that if he were the same age as me then he would have been rather old to go into an orphanage just a few years ago.

"Oh Jill, darling. This is hard enough, and you're not taking me at all seriously," said Mummy, looking very anxious. I began to see this from her point of view. To have carried this secret all these years must have been a heavy burden.

Chapter Two – A Week in Chatton

I couldn't sleep that night. I tossed and turned and tried to find a way of ordering my mind with this new information. Mummy drove me to the train station. I was to travel to Chatton for a few days before flying from London to Sydney. Normally, this would have been the most tremendous adventure. Now it had become a journey to a far land to search for a missing piece of my childhood.

I think that the long train journey helped me get used to this devastating truth. I couldn't help but indulge in daydreams about how my childhood might have been different if only that man hadn't cracked his head and died. But life is full of 'what ifs'. I had to concentrate on the present. Besides, Mummy and I wouldn't have ended up living in a Scottish castle with a magnificent stable complex!

Ann picked me up from the station at Oxford and drove me back to Pool Cottage. She was burbling on about local events, from Mark Lansdowne living at the Farthingtons' in his determined pursuit of Mercedes Pevensy to Susan King and Austin Pevensy's secret dalliance. I listened in silence, nodding and managing to make suitable noises, but for once, my heart wasn't in it. I was thinking about the stranger I had to meet in Australia, who was my father.

Then I was whisked into a drama with the theft of Black Boy from the Ellison-Heath's stable yard. We were dashing around solving the mystery in the best Enid Blyton style, and I could at least put aside my thoughts about my father. That was until shortly before I was due to fly to Australia.

Ann had not been fooled, and she cornered me after supper and forced me to spill the beans. It was a relief to have my beloved Ann to confide in. I knew I could trust her, and she wouldn't tell a soul if I made her promise, crossed her heart and hoped to die.

"What is it about this trip to Australia that has twisted you up Old Bean?" asked Ann, staring straight into my eyes with a laser glance.

I felt like a bomb had fallen and there was a crater in my soul. I began to cry.

"My darling, Jillikins!" exclaimed Ann. "Tell me all. Can it be that bad? What on earth is it?"

"My whole life, I believed something, and it wasn't true! Promise you won't let on to a soul, not even Henry!" I said, my voice dropping to a conspiratorial whisper. "Mummy told me just before I left. I had absolutely no idea."

Ann hazarded a guess that I had been adopted, and this gave me the opening.

"Mummy is my mother, but my father isn't dead!" I announced.

"But where is he?"

"In Australia."

Ann's mouth was agape. She was lost for words and it wasn't often that this happened.

"Why on earth would your mother tell everyone he was dead. Did he run away with a floozy, and she couldn't bear the whispering behind her back?" asked Ann, questions tumbling out once the floodgates were opened.

"He went to prison," I whispered. "Mummy didn't want everyone to know that he was convicted of murder." I explained the circumstances. "I've got a father, an actual real, living, breathing father, and I have no idea what I am meant to think, let alone what I'm meant to feel."

The conversation went long into the night, and I found that this helped. Sometimes, I thought that no problem in the world couldn't be at least half solved with an in-depth discussion with one's best buddy.

On my last day in Chatton, I decided to visit Mrs Darcy's riding school. Mrs Darcy wasn't there. Wendy was busy in the office, but Serena was about to go and ride Patchwork at the Farthingtons'. She invited us to go with her. It was a welcome and entertaining distraction. The sight of Mark Lansdowne, not exactly my favourite person, mucking out the dining room where the horses were kept was amusing.

Mark glowered at us, his eyes glinting under the light of the crystal chandelier. Serena was oblivious to the familial tension and proudly showed off Patchwork, the skewbald horse, showing promise as an eventer. Mark had ridden him to victory at Tiddington Hunter Trials in the novice event. I watched Serena riding Patchwork. She was competent, and the horse seemed to have been trained well.

"Will Mark get the ride after Serena does all the work?" I asked cynically.

"I have no idea," replied Ann. "Let's hope that Serena gets her chance. After all, Mark has his own horses and will probably get his pick of the Pevensys' horses. You know he and Mercedes are now an item. It looks like he's won her heart, and they will draw him into the bosom of their family."

"Well, good luck to them," I commented sardonically. It looked like Mark had landed on his feet after his family had lost all their money.

"Jill, that's not sour grapes?" questioned Ann. "Not like you at all."

I muttered darkly and arranged my face in the semblance of civility. "I really don't care who Mark Lansdowne gets involved with. I felt the ground shifting beneath my feet. Nothing stayed the same.

Chapter Three – Halfway Around the World

The plane roared down the runway, rocking and swaying while it gathered speed. I remembered reading somewhere that most plane crashes occur on take-off. What if I died before I had a chance to meet my father? He would have waited for all these years to meet his only daughter to have her fried in a burning inferno. I shut my eyes, took a deep breath and felt the plane whooshing up into the sky.

All the excitement of going to a new country, showjumping up and down the east coast of the Australian continent, had paled into insignificance with this news. I resented dealing with something like this when I thought I was setting out on the most tremendous adventure. We were in the air now, and all the lurching and swaying stopped. It was like floating on an enormous bubble. I was a princess on a magic carpet.

I could smell cigarette smoke. I was seated in the non-smoking section, but in the confined space, there was no escaping the persistent pungent tang of tobacco. I hoped that I was not going to suffer from air sickness. Vomiting into a small paper bag might be a skill that had to be acquired.

I had been fortunate to have a window seat, but it was difficult to stumble out into the aisle and down to the bathroom. I was seated next to an enormous woman whose layers of fat seemed to bulge over the armrest and invade my own small portion of personal space. She smelt of a very strong perfume, which, mixed with cigarette smoke, was making me feel nauseous.

I turned my head away and looked down at the sea below. Claustrophobia and panic clutched at me, squeezing me as if I were trapped in a tiny space and couldn't escape. I struggled to my feet and climbed over the fat woman and the man beside her and staggered down the aisle. In the bathroom, I splashed tepid water on my face.

Standing in the aisle way, I couldn't bear to clamber back into my tiny seat. The next twenty-four hours stretched before me endlessly. I took a huge breath and turned my mind to think about the Heyward family, who would be meeting me when we landed in Sydney. There were five of them: a mother, a father, two sons and a daughter. The young men would now be twenty-two and twenty-one, and Norah, my own age, was twenty. They had come as paying guests to our castle, and we had got on fabulously.

Norrie and Dorrie Cannon, the famous Australian showjumping twins, were the only two other Australians I had ever known. I had met them during my 'pony jobs' stage before Mummy announced she was getting married and we were moving to Scotland. Mrs York, the godmother of my cousin Cecilia, had put us on to Maud Day, their aunt. Dorrie and Norrie had come over from Australia to visit and rest up before they had a hectic summer of British showjumping. Their aunt hadn't known about their equestrian fame and had innocently arranged for Ann and me to teach them to ride.

We had spent weeks trying to instil the basics of horsemanship. We had thought them to be utter duds as they managed to topple off for no apparent reason while the pony was standing still, and sometimes they fell upon the ponies' necks and clasped their arms around them, crying that they were afraid. We had stayed with them at Mrs Day's pig and chicken farm and were also employed to provide them with companionship. They taught us to ice skate, and they were generally great fun, except for riding. Mysteriously, they had cycled off three afternoons a week. We were about to give up and go home when they announced they wanted to compete in a point-to-point.

Ann and I had been utterly gobsmacked and appalled at this idea. We knew we were not skilled enough to compete in a point-to-point competition ourselves, and Norrie and Dorrie could barely ride, as far as we knew. They told us that a 'friend' would lend them some horses. Shortly before the event, we discovered that they were, in fact, the famous Australian Cannon twins, and we had been duped. They explained that it had all got complicated when their Aunt came up with the idea of them learning to ride, and they were trapped in their own deception. They had performed magnificently at the local point-to-point, and their aunt had told the press that Ann and I had taught them to ride, which, of course, was ridiculous, but we were photographed in the local paper.

This episode was particularly important because Captain Cholly-Sawcutt was present at the event, and we had to explain what had happened. He then delivered a most surprising homily about us getting ordinary non-horsey jobs and having horses as a hobby. This was a hard lump of common sense to swallow. At the time, I was too embarrassed to mention to the Captain that he had promised me a job at his stables some years ago. In fact, I'm not sure why Ann and I hadn't gone and asked him for a job instead of trying out our series of rather bizarre pony jobs. Much later, we discovered that he was in the first stage of dementia at this point and had entirely forgotten his earlier promise. I know many of my dear readers were puzzled by this inconsistency, but the truth was tragic. Now the, Captain has progressed to entirely forgetting who he is and that he had ever ridden for Britain as a showjumper. His stables are being run by his eldest daughter, April and her fiancé, Gary Horton.

I had hoped I might run into the Cannons while on the showjumping circuit. They had spoken with the same sort of accent as the Heywards, sort of long and flat, with a bit of a drawl. I had toyed with the idea of trying to pick up the accent so that I would fit in. I didn't want the Australians to think I was a prissy Britisher with mawkish airs and graces. The Heywards had taught me some Australian phrases, 'don't come to the raw prawn with me', roughly translated as 'don't mess around with me', and 'flat out like a lizard drinking', which meant 'doing something very quickly'. There was another, but I couldn't quite remember it. It was something a little crude about when one was hungry and low-flying ducks.

"As rare as rocking horse poo" and "mad as a meat axe", I exclaimed. The air hostess looked at me and then turned away. She probably encountered all sorts of strange people in her occupation. Gently, she suggested that I return to my seat as we were heading into some turbulence. I clambered back over the two passengers, settled down and shut my eyes. Then, I was assailed by a flood of memories of my father.

We had lived in a white house that was big and rambling at the foot of a hill in Wales. Daddy didn't ride, but he loved horses above all animals. When we went for a walk, he would never pass a field with a horse in it without stopping. He would call the horse, and every time it came to him, he would stroke its nose and talk to it, almost as though he and the horse were communicating.

One day, when my father stroked a horse's nose, a farmer came by and said, "Look-you-now!" (Which is a Welsh way of saying Gosh.) The reason was that this particular horse was supposed to be a nasty creature that its owner couldn't do anything with. But my father could, and that was why the farmer said, "Look-you-now!" So, I naturally grew up with the idea that horses were animals to be fond of.

I had believed that my father was a psychic, or as I had written in my second pony book, *A Stable for Jill*, 'physical'. But then, over the years, I learnt more about horse behaviour, such things as hooded eyes signalling comfort and relaxation, a lowered head indicating submission, and sixteen muscles in their ears to signal all sorts of things.

"Psychic, physical," I mused, my mind starting to wander as I fell asleep.

"I beg your pardon," demanded the fat lady.

"Just thinking aloud" I stuttered, mortified. Being cooped up in a metal cylinder in such close proximity to a bunch of strangers was not a pleasant experience.

I took out my Christmas book, *The Silver Brumby*. I had saved it to read on the plane. The story was set in the mountains in the Australian bush. The names of the plants and the animals were strange, utterly foreign. I felt suspended in an entirely unknown world.

The astonishing news of my father living in Australia had rendered this whole experience unreal. My mind was whirling, and I was finding it hard to put things together in a sensible order. Mummy had told me that the Heywards knew nothing of my father, and it was up to me if I wished to confide in them. It was so odd as I had never missed having a father. It had simply been a fact of life.

Finally, after several stopovers in places around the world to refuel we got to Australia. The plane bounced with a heart-stopping jerk as it hit the runway. Then it settled and spun across the tarmac, slowing to crawl in a curve and halted near the cluster of airport buildings. I could see a set of stairs being wheeled over. Eventually, we stumbled down the aisle, our hand luggage bumping against us, and I was at the top of the steps. The smell of Australia assailed me. Beneath the dominant wave of fuel fumes was a tangy eucalyptus smell in the morning air. I looked across the tarmac into the distance which was slightly hazy with golden dust.

A moment of pure anxiety hit me as I walked across the blistering tarmac towards the airport building. What if the Heywards had forgotten I was coming? I would be alone in this huge, empty, desolate country. I was uncertain what to do and followed behind the herd of passengers. First, we went to collect our baggage. Mummy had thoughtfully tied a big yellow ribbon around the handle of my nondescript brown suitcase. I had raised my eyebrows at this, but now I saw how helpful it was to pick it out of the jumble of other luggage. Every other passenger also seemed to have a brown suitcase. Nonetheless, I quickly untied the ribbon as we progressed towards the officials who were to check our passports and luggage.

The customs officials were looking for contraband, and I felt unaccountably guilty, as if I were trying to smuggle in all sorts of illegal goods. They picked me out of the line, and my suitcase was heaved onto a table and opened. I half-expected it to be filled with guns and ammunition and sighed audibly with relief when all it contained was my clothes, including some rather grey, worn and patched underwear.

The friendly uniformed officer smiled broadly.

"Well, nothing to worry about this young lady." It was the first really Australian accent I had heard in this country.

"Thank you," I said, trying to imitate the laconic drawl. My words came out strangled and breathless. My Australian accent was something I was going to have to work on. I walked on to the exit and heard someone calling my name.

"Jill! Jill!" It was Mrs Heyward. I could have cried at the sight of her. She was accompanied by one of the boys, either Robbie or John.

"Where is Norah?" I asked as we robustly shook each other's hands. The brother took my suitcase, picking it up as if it were a mere matchbox. I imagined that all Australian men were bronzed, strong and healthy – good colonial stock.

"Norah had an appointment and couldn't make it, but she's dying to see you. There are all sorts of plans afoot, including sailing with us on the Harbour," replied Mrs Heyward. "We have the loveliest yacht, billowing white sails. She's called *Blackbird*."

"And horses?" I asked. "Where do you keep the horses?" I was looking at the city roads, houses, shops, and businesses. There seemed to be nowhere to keep and ride a horse in Sydney.

"We've got them at the stables at Centennial Park. They have a super showjumping arena and first-class trainers who keep us on our toes," said the brother who was Robbie, smiling a slow, lazy, wide grin.

"Exactly how many horses do you have?" I asked, unashamedly wanting to know which I would ride and how the showjumping trip was planned.

"We have six!" said Robbie. "That's one for each member of the family and old Misty, who taught us all to ride and can still get around a jump course without disgracing himself."

"Wow!" I echoed. "So, who is going on this trip, the whole family?"

"No," he replied. "Dad has to work at the bank, so it is Mum, me, John, Norah and you."

"That's five of us competing?" I asked, trying to ensure that I would be competing and that I hadn't been invited along to be a groom.

"Mum doesn't want to jump. She's happy to help hold horses while we walk the course, so four of us are riding in the competitions. However, Mum will ride the horses around to help warm them up, and she's taking her young horse to get used to going to shows."

"I've lost the will to jump those huge heights," said Mrs Heyward cheerfully.

"Where will we sleep?" I asked.

"We three girls will sleep in a compartment in the truck, and the boys will camp out on the ground in their swags," replied Mrs Heywood.

"What's a swag?" I asked.

"It's like a canvas bag with a thin mattress and some bedding. It zips up so you're in an envelope that insects and snakes can't get into," said Robbie, grinning at me.

"Snakes!" I said with a delicate shudder.

"We've thousands of snakes in Australia," said Robbie teasingly. I wasn't sure whether to believe him, but I had a sneaking feeling he was telling the truth. I would have to find a book on reptiles and check on the facts. I knew enough about brothers to suspect that teasing the females in the family was their favourite sport.

"Jill, don't let him upset you," said Mrs Heyward soothingly. "Of course, there are snakes. You just have to watch out, look at the ground when you're walking and certainly don't tread on anything that looks like a stick. Don't worry. On average, only two people are killed by snakes every year."

This motherly advice, perhaps designed to reassure me, was more frightening than Robbie's statement!

"Snakes usually hang out around water," piped up Robbie helpfully. So, in long grass around the dam or a river, under the water tank is the most likely place they will be slithering around."

I groaned softly, remembering Mrs McIver from the local shop in Scotland muttering darkly about the 'wee beasties'.

"Whereabouts do you live in Sydney?" I asked.

"Rushcutters Bay, with a view of the harbour," said Mrs Heywood matter-of-factly. I suspected that their house would be grandiose.

"How far is that from the stables?" I asked.

"Takes about ten minutes to drive, depending on traffic," replied Mrs Heywood nonchalantly.

I sat back and watched the cityscape of Sydney flash by, digesting this information. The sky was bright blue, a more intense blue than I had ever seen, and the light was very clear and white. The traffic rumbled restlessly around us, and Mrs Heyward effortlessly changed lanes, overtook and kept her nerve in the confusing flow of vehicles. There were ugly modern shops and red brick apartment buildings all mixed up between sweet terrace houses that looked colonial. I noticed a golden Labrador straining on its leash, pulling along a heavy-set man dressed in shorts and sandals. A slight cool breeze, a salty tang coming off the harbour.

"We're nearly home," said Mrs Heyward. "I hope you like our house, Jill!"

"I can't imagine I won't," I replied politely.

The road had narrowed and wound up a hill. Luxuriant overgrown gardens with long drives led to relatively large houses.

Mrs Heyward indicated, and the big luxurious car slid up a long driveway to a humungous house that stood high on a hillside. The steep driveway led through a Japanese-inspired garden with ponds and carefully arranged plants – serene and cool.

Of course, it wasn't as big as Blainstock Castle, but as far as houses went, it was extremely impressive. It was built like a series of cardboard boxes sitting on top of each other in an elegant pile, with many large windows and a deck that stretched around the first floor.

I got out of the car, suddenly swept with jet lag and feeling very stumbly and weary. There was the fragrant smell of frangipani. The garden was lush and heavy with bougainvillea, and there were sandstone steps up to the front entrance.

Norah was waiting for us, hopping from one leg to another in excitement. I climbed up the steps towards her.

"Look at the view!" she exclaimed when I reached the top, sweeping her hand downhill. "Isn't it wonderful! The house has been built to take advantage of the harbour view."

I turned to survey the vista. It was certainly the most turquoise water I have ever seen, lots of white billowing sails of yachts, cliffs, golden coves and brownish, green scrub along the shore's edge.

"Wow!" I said, genuinely impressed. "It's like living in a postcard!"

Robbie was carrying my suitcase, and we stepped through a large wooden door that opened onto a wide passageway.

I was overcome with the strange sensation that I was neither indoors nor outdoors. There were giant pots with huge fern-like plants curling and spreading on either side. Large paintings hung on the walls in between plants. The floor was polished wooden parquet.

"All the bedrooms are on the third floor," said Norah cheerfully, leaping up the stairs on her thin legs. Although we were the same age, I felt positively middle-aged. My body seemed to have aged twenty years. I struggled behind her and was relieved when we arrived at a large guest bedroom. There was a double bed in the middle of the room, built-in wardrobes and a smooth, modern-looking chest of drawers. A full-length mirror was stuck on the wall.

"You can see the Harbour from here," said Norah, drawing back full-length curtains that framed a large window.

"A lovely view!" I said, not wanting to dim her excitement. I was overcome with fatigue. I slumped down on the bed. I needed to sleep for a week.

"I wanted us to go and see the horses," said Norah, noticing my lack of energy.

"Now, Norah, I think we should let Jill have a rest. It's a mammoth journey, you know. She's been flying for more than twenty-four hours, and it is night time for her now. Let her sleep. There's fruit juice there and biscuits. Just come down when you wake up," said Mrs Heyward from the doorway.

"But Jill, there's so much I want to ask you about Mary Quant, Veruschka, Carnaby Street and King's Road," exclaimed Norah.

"I've shopped on King's Road," I said hesitantly, "but I have no idea who Veruschka is?"

"But she is gorgeous, a German model, so tall and divinely elegant," said Norah, as if she was sure I was part of the in-crowd in London. I don't think she understood that really I was from a small village where the dominant interest was ponies and gymkhanas. Otherwise, I lived in a large castle in the back of beyond.

"I'm sorry," I apologised, feeling distinctly parochial. I lay down on the bed, having carefully removed my shoes and fell into a dead sleep as if I were unconscious. The little clock on my bedside table pointed to twelve o'clock when I opened my heavy lids, hardly remembering where I was. I sat up with a start. What must they think of me to sleep for hours immediately upon my arrival?

I listened, and no sound drifted down the corridor or through the bedroom door. Perhaps they had all gone out? I would venture downstairs and find myself alone in this huge house halfway around the world. I sat up and shook myself mentally. This was not my usual practical, jokey self that forged through life with a zest for adventure. Usually, I was not a young woman who was beset with ridiculous sissy fears.

I got up and went down the passageway and the stairs to find my hosts. On the ground floor, I went into what was probably the living room, which I later learned is more often called the lounge room in Australia. One side of the room had floor-to-ceiling bay windows that looked down at the harbour. Harsh sunlight lit up the sixties modernism with chrome and heavy leather furniture—expensive Persian rugs. What I found quite extraordinary was that one end of the room was sunken—a sizeable square ditch lined with couches. I learned later that this was quite the fashion in Australia. I had never seen such a thing. I slid towards this strange, modern phenomenon when Mrs Heyward appeared in the doorway.

"Oh, Jill dear! You're up. You must be starving. Come into the kitchen. I'll give you a feed."

I smiled at this expression as if I were a horse to be given a bucket of oats.

"I am ravenously hungry," I admitted, following her back down the corridor to the kitchen. It was a large room, as big as the lounge room, with a bench,

stools, and a breakfast bar.

"I was just watching *Mr Ed the Talking Horse*, which is one of my guilty pleasures, indulging in daytime television. Sit down there. Now, a cup of coffee, perhaps. Then there is fruit, cheese, bread, cereal, toast, or perhaps a ham and salad sandwich."

"A cup of coffee would be tops, and anything to eat that is handy," I said.

I looked at the television placed at the end of the kitchen bench for easy viewing while one cooked.

"I've never heard of *Mr Ed*," I admitted.

"It's terribly American, but it is rather amusing. Mr Ed is a horse that talks to his owner, Wilbur. He can even answer the phone. He has a very interesting character."

I watched for several minutes and indeed I could see that it was a compelling, if rather light-weight, programme.

"Norah has gone to the stables to work the horses. I thought once you've eaten, I can take you over. I'm sure you're keen to try out the mounts."

"Oh, rather!" I said enthusiastically. "You've got a tennis court!" I exclaimed, dragging my eyes from the television and looking out the window into the Australian version of a back garden.

"Yes, that's right. It is rather fun. We run a sort of summer tournament for our friends. There is even a rather large Heywards trophy, which is awarded to the winner," she told me.

"What a good idea. I wonder if we should have a tennis court at the Castle," I mused.

I wolfed down several luscious pieces of some sort of tropical fruit, which she placed before me.

"Mango," said Mrs Heyward as if reading my thoughts.

"It's utterly divine," I said, savouring the distinctive sweet flavour.

"We get them in big boxes sent down from our friends in Queensland. That's the state north of New South Wales."

After the fruit, I tucked into a big bowl of muesli, which looked like bird food but was rather delicious, served with icy cold fresh milk. My appetite sated. I was looking forward to seeing these showjumpers.

I returned to my room and changed into my jodhpurs and an Aertex shirt.

"You might want to put on sunscreen," said Mrs Heyward. This Australian sun can be very fierce, and you have such a milky English complexion."

She gave me a tube of sunscreen, and I smeared it on my face.

"And a big shady hat," said Mrs Heyward, handing me an Akubra.

Chapter Four – Australian Showjumping Horses

We drove back through the lush streets that overlooked the Harbour. The bright sunshine wasn't golden like at home, but rather a white empty light stretching up to the blue sky into eternity.

Less than a quarter of an hour driving, we wheeled into a park entrance and went along a driveway to a stable yard. It was spacious, with rows of large loose boxes with high ceilings, all with overhanging roofs that provided extra shade. There was an outdoor arena with showjumps set at about four feet and a big, flea-bitten grey bounding around the jumps. He leapt each of the fences with ease.

"There's Norah!" exclaimed Mrs Heyward.

I walked over to watch. Norah was undoubtedly a good rider, and the horse moved like clockwork. For some reason, I was surprised. I hadn't thought Australians would be so good at our sport. This first realisation shook my belief that the British were the best in horsemanship. I should have known. I had been to Germany and seen how proficient the Germans were at dressage, but somehow, my stoic pride in all things British had survived.

"Jill darling!" Norah drawled, riding over to where I was watching. She spoke with a very good imitation of an aristocratic British accent.

"Oh, Norah!" exclaimed her mother with pursed lips. "That ridiculous accent! You sound like a drongo."

Norah's laugh tinkled through the air, oblivious of her mother's distaste.

I wondered if the accent was some strange adolescent rebellion. Some young people swear and curse, but Norah experimented with different accents. Perhaps she was hoping to become an actress.

Mrs Heyward hurrumphed and walked away, shaking her head.

"He's a very impressive horse," I said, shying away from family tensions.

"Yes, he's your designated mount," said Norah. "We've had him for years. He's one of the best jumpers, so he is to be yours, as you are the guest."

"How terribly kind," I said, feeling embarrassed but at the same time pleased.

"He's seventeen years old, but he still has an amazing turn of speed in a jump-off. His speciality is the six-bar."

"What is a six-bar?" I asked.

"It's a line of six jumps, each higher than the previous one. It is a fantastic spectacle. We like high jumps, seeing which horse can jump the highest."

"That is different to England. How high do you jump?"

"The record is over 8 feet. A horse called Gold Meade jumped eight feet six inches in 1946 and hasn't yet been beaten."

"I can't imagine how any horse and rider could jump that high," I said doubtfully, wondering if I had travelled to a world of superbeings and alien horses.

"Here, have a ride. His name is Captain. We call him Cappie."

I mounted with some difficulty. Of course, Mrs Darcy had taught me how to mount tall horses when I was a callow youth, but this one was over 17 hh. I sprang as best I could and hauled myself up. Norah's stirrup leathers were the same length as I usually rode in. The saddle was very forward cut, and he had a snaffle bit with a drop noseband and a running martingale.

I walked him around the arena. He had a long stride, not exactly smooth, but he confidently covered the ground. We trotted, and I took up the rein, but he didn't like strong contact, so he tossed his head. I used my legs to try to bring him together, but he didn't feel cooperative.

"Take him round the jumps!" shouted Norah impatiently.

I drew a deep breath. I felt as if I had something to prove, to show that I was up to this Australian way of jumping.

I pushed Cappie into a canter, murmuring softly and asking him to be good for me. I found adjusting to his long, raking stride hard, but I knew there was no turning back. I would have to jump him in front of Norah. Undoubtedly, Mrs Heyward would be watching too. Then I saw, to my dismay, that a group of people had gathered around the arena's edge, perhaps curious to watch the Britisher riding.

I cantered two laps trying to collect up the uncooperative Cappie, who had his own ideas of how he liked to go. I could feel no psychic connection with him. I was sure that he despised me and my way of riding.

I wrapped my legs around him and hoped for the best as I rode towards the lowest jump, perhaps only three-foot-six. He seemed to take off half a stride before the point I would have chosen, but he flew into the air confidently, tucked his hoofs beneath him, and there was no risk of hitting the rail.

I turned in a half circle, and we went towards a formidable series of three jumps, one stride between the first and second element, and then three strides on to the third element. I have to admit that Cappie made it easy. He just took his own line and cleared the jumps. I was a mere passenger, but I guess if it worked, that would be how I would ride him.

"Isn't he a fabulous fellow!" exclaimed Norah as I walked back to her and Mrs Heyward. "You two are going to go great guns in the shows."

I dismounted with relief. It had been a harrowing experience. I felt as if I had passed a particularly difficult test.

"Come and see the other horses," urged Norah, taking my hand and towing me towards the loose boxes. "We've decided to retire Misty. We're taking him with us and dropping him off at some friends who have a big property, and he can live out his days there in peace and splendour. So that makes five. Cappie is to be yours, but you can still ride some of the others depending on the events and who will ride what. Although one of them, Dunker isn't yet really jumping, certainly not in competitions."

Mrs Heyward took Cappie's reins, and he followed behind us.

All the Heywards' horses were next to each other in a line of loose boxes shaded by large gum trees. I could smell the sharp eucalyptus scent, and dust rose in clouds beneath our feet as we walked. There was the raucous cawing of birds, which Mrs Heyward informed me were magpies.

"This is Annie," said Norah fondly at the first loose box. "She's my own special horse. We understand each other." She was a tall bay thoroughbred mare with a white blaze. "She has the most beautiful paces. She just floats across the ground, and she can jump anything when she wants to. But she can be a bit precocious; she gets nervous and sometimes twirls in a circle. I think she had a bad experience earlier in life, and I have to be patient with her. On her good days, she is unbeatable."

"Now we have Hussy. Another mare. Only 16 hh, plain chestnut with no white markings - a tough nut. You have to be careful; don't trust her. When she's in a bad mood, she can nip when you turn your back. She's John's horse. She prefers men. She likes a tough rider who won't let her get away with her little nasty tricks. She's a good jumper and can jump anything from a standstill when she wants. Other times, she's got a nasty stop in her."

The next horse was only a pony, perhaps a shade taller, about 14.3 hh.

"I know he's not tall, and Robbie looks a bit ridiculous on him with his long legs, but he is the most amazing jumper. He can turn on a sixpence, and I think he really enjoys winning. He and Robbie can be unbeatable, especially in the Top Score. You know when you take your own line and choose your course, with different jumps worth different points."

I stroked the little dark roan on the nose. He had a lovely, neat head with a concave profile. He probably had Arab blood in him.

"His name is Pepperpot. He was Robbie's pony all through his teenage years when we were in the Pony Club," went on Norah. She led Cappie into the next loose box, and I helped her untack him.

"I like this saddle," I commented.

"It's a Siegfried, a Stubben. We love these German saddles," said Norah, throwing a light fly rug over Cappie's somewhat bony quarters. "I know he's not that fat, but honestly, we feed him all the time. He's regularly wormed. The vet says it's just his natural physique."

"And last but not least is our young horse, he's still in training, we bought him last year. He's a warmblood, a Trakehner. It's the latest thing, these German horses. His name is Dunker, and he's showing a lot of potential with his flat work, but he's still immature. We thought we might just put him in a few hack or riding classes. Apparently, these warmbloods take many years to mature, and he's only five years old."

He was an impressive, tall black horse with a very thick mane and tail. I liked the look of him. I remember this type of horse from working in Germany in a dressage yard.

"We've ridden Cappie, and before you got here, I took Pepperpot for a burl around the park with Mummy on Dunker. That should be enough for today."

Mrs Heyward drove us back to the house. The light began fading into a soft, powdery sapphire blue haze – the harbour and the sky melting together. A warm breeze was blowing. It was quiet except for the tinkle of rigging wires on the yachts in Rushcutters Bay. This suburb was filled with houses with inheritance views. The wind blew up. A ferry horn sounded. Darkness had fallen, and lights came on some of the boats moored in the bay. The stiffening westerly breeze had pushed their bows in a uniform direction – all facing down the harbour into the wind.

Dinner was served on the back verandah that evening. It struck me as I sat down at the table that growing up with such a big family was very different from my upbringing, which was just Mummy and me. There was an endless stream of banter from Norah and Robbie. The Heywards prided themselves on getting on with things. Any negative emotions, uncertainty or unhappiness, were submerged in the hidden depths of an ocean while the family members bobbed around in colourful boats on the surface bathed in the sunshine of eternal cheerfulness. Resilience was celebrated. I compared this to my life with Mummy. It's not that she and I spent our days maundering on the negative side of life, but we did express ourselves when we felt unhappy. There was just a two-way dynamic between us. Here, the five family members clashed and clattered against each other, and there was a constant noise.

Although the three children all conformed to the family culture of jolly good sense and calm acceptance that life was good, they were in themselves a study in contrasts. Although the boys, really young adults, were physically similar, tall, well-muscled, healthily tanned, keen blue eyes and wide, full-lipped mouths, Robbie was a livewire, a joker, and John was more serious about life and the pursuit of achievement. Norah was tall and slim, with thick, curly, dark-brown hair, and her blue eyes were large and shining. She was living her life up in the air, in a world of dreams and ideas, longing for a life full of romantic adventures.

"You're all so tall," I said randomly as everyone sat.

This inane comment was taken cheerfully.

"It must be so cosy to be short," said Norah, "but we've got long genetics in our family."

Mrs Heyward had an air of efficiency and no-nonsense that would have suited her to the role of a headmistress. She was tall and slim with well-cut brown hair that curled slightly and shone with a reddish tinge. Mr Heyward seemed to revel in his role as a city banker who provided his family with every good thing, from a stable of six horses, a yacht and the best fee-paying education available in Sydney. He was an older, sturdier version of his sons.

The food served was utterly delicious. The abundance of fresh fruit and vegetables meant a salad far beyond the usual lettuce leaf and slice of tomato that constituted such fare in England. There were bean shoots, bamboo shoots, raw mushrooms, endives, fresh herbs grown in pots on the verandah, crispy yellow peppers and three different types of lettuce. There was thick Scotch fillet steak that was barely seared and served very rare with three kinds of mustard and crusty bread that they called damper, an Australian name for a type of bread usually cooked on a campfire.

Mr Heyward was talking about some work being done on the yacht. It had gone in for hull cleaning, and much of the woodwork was being revarnished. They asked me about my sailing experience, and I had to admit it was limited to sailing the small boats on the loch. They promised to take me out on the harbour after we returned from showjumping. I showed suitable enthusiasm for the idea.

A lot of the time, my mind was worrying over the coming meeting with my father. Otherwise, this holiday would have been one long, jolly charabanc ride. Perhaps I would enjoy everything more once I had finished the meeting. I had pondered on whether Mummy should have simply written him out of my life, telling me he was dead, but I thought that, on balance, she had been right. To say that it would have been a stain on the family escutcheon was a severe understatement, 'a convicted murderer'. Not that Mummy and I had a family escutcheon *per se*. I couldn't bear to imagine what the gossips in Chatton would have made of that when I was growing up. The thought of the taunts and jeers of Susan Pyke (now King) and her cronies when I was at school was unbearable.

Chapter Five – Training on Cappie

The next morning was relentlessly sunny with a cloudless blue sky. I woke and looked out the window. Although totally open windows weren't a thing in Australia. They all had fly screens, mesh that prevented the flies from swarming in. The salty tang of the sea gusted in on the breeze. We were to ride this morning and it would be a proper training session. I was glad of this as I was anxious to have as much practice as possible before we set off on the show circuit. Riding an unknown horse, the tremendous heights of the jumps and the differences in competition types were a challenge that I hoped I could rise to.

The Heyward family were congregated in the kitchen, sitting at a big table set with a wonderful range of food. There was a large bowl of fresh fruit salad which had to be at least half mango, also watermelon balls, sliced peaches, apricots and seedless green grapes. Such an exotic mixture of fresh fruit was a treat that we rarely enjoyed in Britain. There was also toast, fried bacon and eggs, mushrooms and sausages. I had everything. I would need my strength today.

When we arrived at the stables all the boxes had been mucked out. The horses' coats were shining and they looked ready for action. Little flies buzzed around my face and my right hand was constantly in motion waving them away.

"Do they spend the whole day in their stables?" I asked. I couldn't see any paddocks where they might be turned out.

"After they're exercised, we hose them down and they go out into those yards under the trees," explained Norah.

She showed me the saddle rack where Cappie's brown jumping saddle sat, beautifully cleaned and supple, smelling of saddle soap, and a plain brown leather bridle with a snaffle bit, a drop noseband and a rather fancy browband with a green and white design, which matched his spotless padded saddle blanket which was white with green binding. I was most impressed with the standard of tack cleaning. Not even Mrs Darcy, who owned the riding school in Chatton, could have found fault.

I wanted to get to know Cappie well as he was to take me around the mountainous courses that I had to face. I was determined not to disgrace my country. Not that I was actually riding for Britain, but in an informal way I felt as if I were an ambassadress.

Cappie stood quietly and patiently while I saddled him, although when I tightened the girth, he blew himself up and pinned back his ears.

"It's alright, old chap, I'm not going to pinch your skin," I said soothingly. I led him out into the yard and stepped up to the mountain block to get on. I gave him a long rein and walked around the perimeter of the area. I watched as Norah led out her bay mare Annie. She was a good-looking animal with a white blaze but she wasn't self-confident. She minced and sidled and stared intently at anything that moved around her. She behaved as if she had had some nasty shocks in the past and didn't trust the world or anyone in it. Norah was very patient with her. Not a cross word passed her lips, she murmured reassuringly and then mounted and walked over to us.

"Annie and Cappie are friends. He helps her to cope, particularly if we're not at home. She's worse in an unfamiliar environment," she explained.

Norah was right. Annie clung to Cappie, her body curved against him. Almost as if she wanted to crawl into his skin for safety.

Robbie was leading Pepperpot out into the yard. He was much smaller than the other horses, standing at only 14.3 hh. But what he lacked in stature he more than made up for in high spirits. He looked very brave and eager, as if he would stop at nothing. Robbie was tall and vaulted into the saddle with barely a leap. His legs hung down below Pepperpot's stomach but when it came to showjumping looks were not important. The little roan gelding stepped out, brimming with confidence and eager to get going.

"Robbie likes Pepperpot. Mummy wanted him to have a new horse, but he has resolutely refused. He says he will never give up his favourite little dynamo."

John was riding Hussy.

"Watch out for that mare. You know what they say about chestnut mares, well it's totally true with Hussy. Just don't get within striking distance," warned Norah.

"Come on you lot, let's get into the arena and trot and canter some circles to get these horses properly warmed up," instructed John, who liked to take charge.

Obediently we followed him through the gate, all keeping our distance. I gathered up the reins and pushed Cappie on with my legs. He responded only half-heartedly, as if he was thinking, I've been doing this all my life, there's no need for you to make the effort.

The jumps were set up with five sizeable obstacles: a double with three strides between the elements set at about four feet, a triple bar with a huge spread standing at about five feet, a hogsback with a water dish below it, the water glinting in the sun, and a road closed sign set at an angle. That was the one that looked the trickiest. I don't know why but plank type jumps seemed to get knocked more often than any other type of jump.

"First over the double, for a warmup," commanded John. "I'll go first, then Robbie, Jill and Norah as Annie will follow Cappie to the ends of the earth."

We were cantering now, and I adjusted myself to the long loping stride of Cappie and decided that I would leave it all to him but prepare myself for a take-off much earlier than what I was used to.

John and Hussy went over competently but she swished her tail constantly as if she was not best pleased. She really was a very disagreeable mare. Pepperpot bounced over as if he were skipping. Cappie cantered towards the jump and took off a shade earlier than I would have liked but not too much, as if he knew that he had to leave room for two good strides before the second element. He was amazingly easy to ride once you got accustomed to his ways and I began to feel quietly confident.

"Now let's try and do a little course," said Robbie, obviously determined to exert his will and not be constantly instructed by his elder brother. "I think we should do the double, then left circle and over the water jump, gallop towards the triple and then pull them together to take some care over the road closed. I'll go first. I'm the pathfinder." I'm sure he said this just to annoy John and not let him have it all his own way.

He set off on the brave little Pepperpot and skimmed around the course, leaping every obstacle with a judicious six inches clearance, showing off with turns on the haunches instead of arcing around the curves and after a very convincing clear round he galloped across an imaginary finishing line. John watched with his lips pressed together. There was obviously a strong element of brotherly competitiveness here.

"Robbie and John are always adversarial like this," Norah told me by way of explanation. "I've got no time for this ridiculous competitiveness. I put it down to their private schooling."

"Have you turned into a communist?" demanded John, overhearing her comments.

"A socialist," she retorted. "Not that you would know the difference!"

"I'm planning on a political career, so of course I know the difference!" he retorted.

John took off on Hussy, kicking her into a fast canter, jolting her out of her natural rhythm with his bad temper. She took off too late over the first element of the double and came in so close to the second that she hit it with her forelegs. Stumbling slightly on landing and performing a clumsy circle to the left going wide to try and recover herself. She baulked slightly as the morning sun shone off the surface of the water making it hard to judge the height of the poles. John was determined to keep going and pushed her hard into the triple which she cleared, stretching herself over the wide spread. Then, he hauled her in and took exaggerated care to set her up for the road closed which she cleared. He pulled her up to a trot, refusing to copy Robbie's flourishing gallop finish.

"You boys!" taunted Norah.

Robbie laughed but John looked like thunder.

"We just want to get round safely," I murmured to Cappie, not letting myself get drawn into the battle for supremacy. Cappie shook his head slightly, as if agreeing with me. He was too old and wise for any sort of energy-sapping one upmanship. He would save himself for the real thing when we were in a proper competition. After John and Robbie had replaced the rail on the second element of the double we set off. Cappie jumped like clockwork with very little direction from me. I was learning to adapt to his independent style and sat quietly in the saddle.

"Oh, well done, old chap!" said Norah, in her imitation English accent.

She followed around on Annie. She had to hold her strongly as they approached the water jump as the nervous mare didn't like the water tray, but they got round clear.

"Now we'll put everything up six inches," announced Robbie, who was totally confident on Pepperpot who was one of the best jumpers in the yard.

He and John went round and raised the rails. Norah and I held their horses.

"After this round we should have done enough," Norah said to me. "I want to go over to Manly to see Michael. I just have to persuade Mummy. I've got an idea. It's a snorter. I'm going to say I want to show you the sights and take you to the beach."

I realised that this Michael must be the unsuitable young man who Mrs Heyward was concerned about. I didn't imagine for one minute that Norah's mother would be fooled by this excuse. However, it would be enlightening to meet him to see what all the fuss was about. I was unversed in the ways of anti-establishment rebels and by all accounts Norah was enmeshed in a passionate entanglement.

The boys finished adjusting the jumps and remounted. Mrs Heyward appeared mounted on Dunker. She had been hacking him around the park.

"I see that you're all training seriously," she said approvingly.

I noted her riding position and saw that she sat very well. The young Trakehner was an impressive horse.

"Is he going to be a jumper, or are you going to try dressage on him?" I asked when she rode up beside me.

"Well, we'll let him do a bit of jumping but mainly it's flatwork. I've got a young woman coming over twice a week to train him and then give me some instruction. But we're taking him on the show circuit to get him used to travelling and attending events with other horses. We might enter him for some riding classes, just so he gets used to working in an arena with other horses and an audience. You could take him in a riding class," she added as an afterthought. "It would be good for him to experience another rider."

"That would be great," I said. I had been wondering if I might get to have a ride on him. He was a beautiful horse.

"Now you boys no silly business, you understand," she said sternly to her two sons.

"Yes Mum," said John sheepishly. Robbie glowered but didn't argue.

We all went round the course again. Pepperpot did his usual flying clear round. John rode Hussy more sensibly and she got round. I didn't think much of her. She had no panache. Her bad temper seemed to get the better of her all the time. Cappie went clear and so did Annie who was more settled now and barely faltered when it came to the water jump.

"Let's see them relax a bit," said Mrs Heyward. Obediently, we rode around a small area of the park to warm down and then went back to hose the horses in the wash bay. They seemed to love the cool water. We scraped them off and took them over to the sand roll before they were installed in their day yards under the shade of the tall gum trees. They were protected from the irritating flies with light rugs and fly veils attached to their headcollars. They could even reach each other over the rails so they could indulge in a little mutual grooming. Each of them had a full haynet and fresh water.

"These horses have the life of Riley," I said, admiring the way in which they were cared for.

"Only the best for our equine friends," said Mrs Heyward. I saw then that she was a true horse person.

Chapter Six – The Unsuitable Young Man

"Mum," said Norah in a faintly wheedling tone, "I would really like to take Jill around to see some of the sights of Sydney. She's got to get to the beach. Would you take us to Circular Quay? We can catch the ferry over to Manly."

Mrs Heyward looked at her darkly.

"You mean you want to go and visit that questionable young man."

"He's not questionable, he's a poet," replied Norah, her eyes suddenly dreamy with love.

"I haven't got my bathers with me," I said uncertainly.

"That's alright. I've got a couple of bikinis. You can wear one of mine."

"A bikini!" I exclaimed.

"Don't look so shocked. They're perfectly legal these days. I have a very stylish red one that will look great on you," said Norah casually. "Mum, can you drop us off at Circular Quay? After all, Jill needs to do a bit of sightseeing, and a ferry trip across the Harbour will be a treat for her."

Mrs Heyward looked tight-lipped but agreed to drive us.

Norah smirked. I felt most uncertain about wearing a bikini. It seemed extremely racy, and I feared I would be far too staid and old-fashioned to sport such an outfit. I wasn't in the habit of wearing red; I preferred bright blues and green, but the colour was not what concerned me.

I sat in the car's back seat and looked out at the Sydney streets. Green and yellow trams slid up and down the middle of the road.

"This is Woolloomooloo," said Norah.

"How do you spell that?" I asked incredulously.

She just laughed at me.

"I love it. It's like a real place, Unlike hoity toity Double Bay."

I wasn't sure what this meant. I was not *au fait* with the Australian standards of class.

The midday air was hot. The scent of frangipani tinged the air with notes of oil-stained bitumen and cement - the smell of Sydney. A couple were sitting on wooden chairs outside a terrace house. They were wearing bright yellow, green and blue clothes, not the English people's usual grey and brown garb.

We were dropped off at Circular Quay and boarded one of the big ferries that carried people across the Harbour. Manly was located on a peninsula. Norah explained that it was a suburban community that loved sport and the outdoors. Many top sports people lived there, surf lifesavers, swimmers, rugby league players and the very latest thing was iron men. This was a sport that had only just begun and involved a combination of swimming, board paddling, ski paddling and running.

The wind was fresh, and tiny white clouds scudded across the sky high above our heads. The land curved around in bays and points on either side of us as the ferry chugged across the dark blue ocean that lapped and swirled against the bow that ploughed through the water.

"You know Sydney Harbour is one of the deepest seaports in the world. Look! Over there!" cried Norah, flinging her arm out. "Sydney Harbour Bridge, it's called The Coat Hanger."

"Let me see!" I said, turning. It was just as it looked in the photos I had seen. An iron construction shaped like an intricate coat hanger spanning the water, linking one piece of land to another.

The ferry chugged along towards the open sea beyond the headlands, and then we turned up the coast to get to Manly. It was like a holiday town. Shops selling ice creams, plastic buckets and spades, brightly coloured bathers and beach towels, and large striped umbrellas lined the streets.

"I've arranged for Michael to meet us down at the beach," said Norah in a conspiratorial voice.

"I thought there was something about you," I said.

"What do you mean?" she asked, giving me a look that suggested I was a bit strange.

"It's as if you're living life on a higher level, something exultant and exciting," I replied slowly. "So, tell me about Michael."

I had been thinking about being in love, and one of the factors I noticed was that people who are in love want to talk about the objects of their adoration all the time. For the brief time of first being in love, their whole world revolves around that one person that they think defines the meaning of their existence. I looked at the Manly people and imagined that this Michael was a superb specimen of Australian manhood: tanned, fit, sun-bleached blonde hair, piercing blue eyes and an awe-inspiring athletic physicality. I vaguely wondered whether he rode, perhaps not, or indeed, he would have been hanging around the stables with Norah. Manly didn't look like the natural habitat of horses and riders.

Norah dragged me into a toilet block, producing the red bikini from her bag. I looked at it dubiously. There didn't seem to be much to it; skimpy.

"Jill! Hurry up! Let's get on! We'll get changed, and then we'll hit the beach."

I took a deep breath and shut myself in a cubicle. I didn't fancy stripping off in the changing room where other women seemed to be carelessly flinging off their clothes with no regard for modesty. I struggled like a contortionist in the small space and managed to arrange the items around my body. Thank goodness I wasn't fat! However, I was very pale, and I thought I would stick out like a colourless ghost amongst this host of sun-tanned Australians.

Norah also had put on a bikini and, over that, a billowy cotton dress decorated in embroidery and tiny mirrors that flashed and sparkled. Her riding clothes were in a plastic bag.

I wrapped the large beach towel around my body and bundled my clothes, including my riding boots, into another plastic bag that Norah handed me. Then, I stepped timidly outside. Norah was on tenterhooks and not at all concerned about my feelings or how I looked, and I found myself following in her wake. My bare feet were burning on the golden sand. I felt like one of those Pacific fire-walkers. I was ready to throw caution to the wind and dash across the dry sand and straight into the waves with their creamy curling foam. Such a mass of frothy whiteness looked like the manes of giant horses. At least in the water, my body would be hidden, and my feet would be cool. I hated being such a spectacle and imagined everyone staring at me.

"Look, there's the umbrella!" said Norah, pointing to a poisonous green and virulent yellow-striped canopy. I imagined that Michael would be there with a cohort of other tanned athletic friends, and I was amazed when we finally arrived at the scene of our meeting place.

Michael was sitting alone, almost cowering in the shade, looking more out of place and white-skinned than me. He was an incongruous figure, and I thought perhaps we had mistaken the umbrella, and this wasn't the marvellous Michael.

He was tall and thin with long, curly black hair, wearing scruffy denim jeans and a long-sleeved t-shirt. I looked at him closely, searching for why Norah found him so fascinating. Perhaps it was his difference. His complexion was more blanched than mine. He smiled up at us, and his brown eyes shone with a winsome charm. Perhaps there was something to him after all.

Norah flung herself at him in a madly unrestrained way. Obviously, she wasn't playing hard to get.

"Michael is a poet!" she declared to me.

She had mentioned this before, and I wondered a little about it. I know that Royce Pevensey wrote poetry but in an understated, terribly English way. He certainly didn't introduce himself as a poet. He was a gentrified farmer who didn't announce to the world his poetic inclinations. I'd never met anyone who labelled themselves as a poet. I was a writer, but I rarely defined myself in this way until I was pushed to declare what I did. I didn't really think that a poet was a legitimate occupation. Most poets only became famous and successful after they were dead. Claiming to be a living poet seemed rather audacious.

"I'm Jill," I said, holding out my hand as if we were in a drawing room, not a wind-swept public beach with lots of brown, almost-naked bodies lounging nearby.

"Good to meet you," said Michael in carefully modulated tones with only a hint of an Australian twang. "I believe you live in a castle which sounds fab. I've been dreaming of living in an old ancestral home forever."

This was to become our point of connection. Michael was beset with medieval, olde-world dreams of a chivalrous persona that didn't exist in Australia's bright, sunny modern world.

"How is the poem going?" asked Norah.

"I fear I've finessed it beyond redemption," sighed Michael.

"Why don't you go in for a swim, Jill?" suggested Norah. "Don't forget to stay between the flags so that the lifesavers can keep an eye on you."

I took the hint that she wanted to be alone with her paramour. I was only too happy to walk across the golden sand and into the cool, undulating and crashing waves. The water was deliciously fresh, and the feeling of the waves sweeping over me and then drawing me back out to sea was like nothing I had ever experienced before. I could see the surfers not far away in the next section of the water. They balanced on their long wooden boards. I did hope that when they came off, their boards wouldn't shoot towards me and hit me on the head.

I noticed people riding the waves with their bodies and tried copying them. You had to go beyond where the waves were breaking and launch yourself as the water swelled upwards and got carried in towards the shore. It wasn't easy, but it was certainly a delicious challenge. Eventually, I decided that I'd better return to the beach and surely Norah and Michael had chirped at each other like lovebirds for long enough. I walked dripping back to the green and yellow umbrella. Norah was stretched prone in the sand beside Michael, who, true to his occupation, was scribbling in a notebook.

I wrapped myself in the towel and sat in the shade of the umbrella.

"We're going to the coffee shop," said Norah. "It's where Michael's friends meet up."

"That sounds good," I said, suddenly ravenous after my swim realising that we hadn't had any lunch. Hopefully, there would be delicious cakes to go with the coffee. I wasn't sure about putting on my jods and riding boots.

"You could just wear your white shirt over the bikini and go barefoot," said Norah, divining my worries about suitable clothing. I must admit I felt only half-dressed, but at least I would fit in with everyone else. I remembered how Susan Pyke made fun of me when I was an eleven-year-old kid and I had first started riding my pony, Black Boy. I had no riding clothes, and she publicly mocked me for wearing a blue and white spotted cotton frock, no hat or stockings, and sandals. Wearing the right clothes was important, and I decided I would have to go shopping and buy some suitable casual wear for the beach and a pair of thongs, which were rubber slip-on shoes with a strap that fitted between one's big toe and the next.

The coffee shop was suitably bohemian, with benches to lounge on with brightly coloured cushions and low coffee tables. We joined a bunch of young people holding court at the back of the room. There were about a half dozen of them. The men had long hair like Michael's, and the girls wore bohemian gipsy outfits. They were smiling and laughing, gesticulating, smoking cigarettes dangled elegantly from their fingers. It struck me that they looked like revellers at a medieval-style carnival. Norah greeted everybody with casual enthusiasm. Seeing her with people away from her family, I realised she scattered her glitter wherever she was. Certainly not suffering from being dependent on the good opinion of other people. She happily believed the people she met and liked would like her equally.

I ordered myself a large lamington, a cube of cake dipped in chocolate sauce and then rolled in coconut. It was delicious. I forgot about feeling embarrassed and munched on my treat.

I sat on the edge of the group, which was deep in conversation. Their voices were a curious mixture of Australian accents and Americanisms. They were discussing a new magazine that they were putting together. I gathered that it was to feature their own contributions. Michael was indubitably the leader of the band. His charisma hovered over the group like a miasma. He sat there pulling on his wispy beard, sometimes giggling, a funny rippling sound. I noticed small details about him, like his narrow, birdlike neck. He was the Head Elf of a funny band of human-type woodland creatures, a compelling personality. I understood now Norah's devotion. She sat beside him, gazing up at him like an adoring nymph. She was in a dream of love.I have been pondering the whole falling in love thing lately, in a general sense, but also particularly concerning Frank Stabley. I had always admired him in my teenage years when he was older and well-respected as a local showjumper. Our evening together eating pizza had been a salutary experience. Of course, we had talked about horses, and the conversation had flowed easily, but I was conscious of the faint stirrings in my soul. Was he 'the one'? The man who would be my husband, soulmate, companion for life? It had all been restrained, unlike Norah's obvious outpouring of total devotion. Her feelings for this Michael made me feel uncomfortable but at the same time I found them fascinating.

"Have you got some advertisers?" I asked, determined to join in the conversation. I had written several articles for *Horse and Hound* and felt I had some grip on the subject. They stared at me. Perhaps literary magazines didn't stoop to such sordid commercial depths.

"What sort of company would want to advertise in our magazine?" Michael asked.

I thought about it. I couldn't really come up with an answer.

"Some product that might appeal to your readers?" I suggested uncertainly. "Perhaps something related to fashion?" was my only lame idea.

"Yes," said one of the girls. "My friend makes these gorgeous skirts, indicating a multi-coloured gathered skirt with little sequins and buttons sewn onto it. I'm not sure whether she might want to advertise." This girl was called Lara. She looked like an exotic goddess with wild blonde hair and sea-blue eyes. When she spoke, you could sense her intelligence.

Then, the conversation went back to the merits of some of the poetic contributions and then the evils of colonialism.

"The social elite are sticking to their colonial ideals," declared one of the girls.

I was content to sit silently on the edge of the discussion. I didn't know why colonialism was evil. Perhaps I would ask Dinah Dean when I returned to Oxfordshire, although I would then be subjected to a diatribe.

The conversation flashed back and forth, and then they laughed uproariously at some recent events related to *Oz*. I had no idea what *Oz* was. Then, there was a magazine passed around with pointed fingers. It got to me, and I turned the pages carefully, almost as if they were an incendiary device. This was actually quite close to the truth. The coverage related to censorship, homosexuality, and something called the White Australia Policy. For me, this was hot stuff. I had never seen anything like it.

Apparently, those involved had been charged with publishing obscene literature.

This group of artistic people did not fit my idea of Australian stereotypes. Norah explained later that they had all gone to private school and were the literary ones. They lived privileged lives and commercial concerns were considered for people with a lower form of consciousness.

The effort of adjusting to hanging out with a group of people totally different from my usual crowd overcame me. I was swept with a wave of exhaustion. My personal clock was twelve hours behind, and it was four in the morning when I should have been fast asleep.

"We'll have to go home now," said Norah to me. "I promised Mummy we would be there for dinner."

As we boarded the ferry back to Circular Quay, the sun was low in the sky. The reflection of the golden orb slipping towards the far horizon reflected in the sea. The waves slapped against the sides of the big boat as it chugged towards its destination.

"It was interesting to meet Michael," I said, standing at the rail beside Norah. "I believe that they are part of the *avant-garde* intelligentsia." I had picked up this phrase from a magazine while sitting in a dentist's waiting room.

"Poets are usually susceptible to self-doubt, but Michael is confident of his artistic destiny. He has armour-plated self-esteem," she replied dreamily. "Unfortunately, Dad says that they're unrepentant and flamboyant, all communists and shiftless artists, indulging in all the pleasures of life with hardly a thought for anything else. I must remember that phrase, '*avant-garde* intelligentsia.'"

"But what should they repent of?" I asked.

"Who knows," she replied. "Come on, we're about to dock. We'd better hurry. We're going to be late for dinner."

After the family meal, Norah came into my room. She seemed to have chosen me as her confidante. In this family of active, outgoing people she needed someone to do the deep and meaningful thing.

"Michael is such a bundle of contradictions. He's shy but an exhibitionist, sensitive but outrageous, old-fashioned but modern, earnest but ironic. He can talk to anyone on any level," she mused.

"How does he get on with your brothers?" I asked, wondering how far Michael's power of connecting with all sorts went.

"They haven't met him. No one in the family has. Mum knows about him, but she hasn't suggested that they meet. I think she wants to brush it under the carpet and just hope it goes away," admitted Norah. "Dad wouldn't want to meet him, just thinks he knows his *type*."

"Do you think they won't get on?" I asked in a neutral tone.

"I can feel the weight of their disapproval before it even gets to a meeting," sighed Norah.

"It's very romantic," I said carefully, "but what sort of life would you have with Michael? I mean, if you're thinking of a future with him." Perhaps settling down and marriage was too conventional for people like Michael and his cohort of poets.

"I dream about us going to Paris to live in an attic. I'm good at French, and I've always wanted to go to Paris," said Norah dreamily, obviously dizzy with bliss.

It seemed a quite conventional daydream, living in a garret in Paris and writing poetry.

"Ernest Hemingway lived in Paris at the beginning of his career. He wrote a book about it," she continued. "I can imagine the Seine flowing like silky caramel between stone walls, green sunlight shining in the trees and street artists exhibiting their paintings."

I realised then that Norah was very educated, an intellectual. She knew about writers and literature. Far more than I did, and I was supposed to be the writer. She lived amongst a big, lively family. Finding Michael, who, other than her straightforward conventional family, had allowed her to express her artistic side.

"Have you talked to Michael about the future?" I asked, wondering where such a relationship could go.

"Only in my mind. I imagine he will say that we won't act out conventional husband-wife roles, that we'll be real."

This seemed indeterminate to me. I began to think about Ann and Henry. They were planning a very conventional life together. Neither Ann nor I had ever questioned falling in love, getting married, and having children who would go to pony club. Perhaps there was another modern world coming that would open the way to other kinds of being. It made my brain tired to think of all these possibilities.

Chapter Seven – On The Road

Norah met up with Michael once more before we set out on our showjumping tour. She dragged me along. We had told her mother that we were shopping for clothes for me that were more suitable for the hot Australian summer. At this meeting, I became uncomfortably aware of the sexual tension between Norah and Michael. Unlike the convivial, comfortable atmosphere between Ann and Henry, this was tangible and obvious.

Michael was dressed in a very hippy style with an embroidered waistcoat and a pair of striped baggy drawstring trousers. He was excited and told us about a trip his friends, and he planned to go to a Greek island. He did not clearly express a wish for Norah to join them. I looked at her sharply, but she continued to smile benignly. I wondered just what degree of commitment had been agreed between them.

Afterwards, Norah said to me, "His smile is like music. Can you hear it?"

"Not exactly," I said, not wanting to negate her illusions. I could understand the power that the young man exuded, but I also found him rather frightening. There was a heedlessness about him, as if he were careless about other people's lives.

"He's told me that his ancestors were Russian aristocracy," she said, eyes alight with innocent worship.

"Do you believe him?" I asked, unable to disguise the hint of scepticism in my voice.

"But of course," she said, looking shocked at my cynicism. "Why would he lie? Can't you feel that there is something different about him? Remember how he connected with you about the Scottish castle? He asked me all about it when I mentioned it. He wanted to know every detail."

"Yes, he's certainly different," I agreed. Privately, I thought he wanted to know every detail of Blainstock Castle because he would use the information to incorporate it into the narrative of his European connections. I wondered how far Norah's love for him was reciprocated. He seemed to like her and treated her well, sometimes in an exaggerated old-world courtesy way, but I sensed an element of playacting in his behaviour.

I thought it was good that Norah was coming away with us. I wondered if a little distance might give her more clarity regarding this beguiling man who had cast a spell on her.

We set off early in the morning. John had taken charge of the arrangements and compiled several lists of equipment. He had carefully packed the truck with all manner of camping, feed and horse paraphernalia. The six horses were loaded, each tripping up the ramp obligingly. Australian horses seemed as laid back as the citizens.

The truck had two bench seats, and Robbie took the first turn at driving. John sat beside him with a map, giving directions on how to get through a maze of roads onto the highway that led south to Bowral. Norah, Mrs Heyward and I sat in the back seat.

Usually, I love the beginning of a trip with all the excitement and diversion ahead of us, but this time, the experience was overlaid with anxiety about meeting my father. I spoke to Mrs Heyward privately, and she agreed to keep my secret. We were to tell the others that I was visiting an old family friend. After the Bowral show, we would stay with the Cosgroves at a large property near Goulburn. This was where Misty was to enjoy a peaceful retirement. Robbie was to borrow one of the station cars and drive me to the small town of Corryong, where my father lived in a cottage with five acres.

I had written to him and told him of the date of my arrival and proposed that I stay three days and three nights before someone returned to pick me up. The morning before our departure, I received a postcard from him, "Can't wait to meet you! D." The 'D' could have been David, or it could be Daddy. We would have to sort out how we stood with each other, even knowing what to call him.

I put all this out of my mind and watched out the window, taking in my first sight of the Australian countryside. There were wide yellow paddocks which shimmered in the heat below the blue sky, and then there were patches of what they call bush — grey and brown straggly trees with dusty green leaves and scrubby bushes.

I mused about the Heyward family now that I had experienced them as real people and not just an Australian family, as I had thought of them before. They were clannish and there was something insular about them. Norah was very close to her brothers, but a rift had developed since her relationship with Michael. Robbie and John were also privately educated but sporty, obsessed with cricket, rugby, sailing and horse riding. They were manly and masculine without any trace of Michael's impish charm.

Despite their adventurous sporting activities, they conformed to society. They attended university to follow in their father's footsteps to work in the banking industry. Although Robbie had occasional aspirations to be a politician, so he was studying law to hedge his bets. They had none of

Michael's rebellious tendencies. I hadn't wanted to ask Norah, but I feared that Michael had delved into the world of illicit drugs. His dilly bag that he slung from his shoulder had a marijuana leaf embroidered patch sewn onto it. On his notebook cover was written, 'Tune in, turn on, drop out.' Michael's happy life on the edge of society frightened me, not for myself but for Norah. I feared that her judgement was flawed and that she could find herself in very deep.

The Heyward children had a great deal of freedom to explore the world. They had travelled to Europe with their parents. But there was not a lot of freedom of expression. They were not encouraged to play with ideas and concepts that went beyond the bounds of their privileged and conventional world.

After a couple of hours, we rolled into Bowral. It was a small country town. Pretentious, if you can say that about a town. It was proud of its old-fashioned brick buildings that stated that the townspeople were solid citizens. Signs were pointing down the road to the outside of the town centre where the showgrounds were.

When we arrived there was a hive of activity. There were two rings, a main one and a smaller one. There were trailers loaded with the makings of showjumps. There were rows of bunting being strung up, and someone said 'testing 1, 2, 3' over the loudspeaker.

"Did you know that Karl Jurenak, a Hungarian is based in this town training the Australian showjumping Olympic team?"

"Really!" I exclaimed. Australia was more international than I had thought.

"Kevin Bacon is famous here in Australia. But it's not just his acrobatic style where he puts no weight on the horse's back as they're in the air. He rides with his feet fully in the irons and his reins bridged."

I smiled at the thought of what Mrs Darcy would say about this.

"Bowral is also famous for its picnic races. Back in the 1930s, people flocked down from Sydney to attend. They were a highlight of the racing and social calendar."

We followed the signs to truck parking.

"I've booked us stables," said Mrs Heyward. "They've given us these numbers 43, 44, 45, 46, 49, 50 and 51."

"That's not consecutive," said John.

"No, dear," said Mrs Heyward as if she had been subject to John's pedantic attention to detail before.

We drove over to the stable area. They weren't exactly stables but a series of long low sheds with partitions that divided them into spaces the size of large loose boxes. We found the numbers of our yards and unloaded the horses. I took charge of Cappie, who behaved like a wise old gentleman who had been through this routine hundreds of times. I was finding it hard to forge a connection with the old horse. It was as if he had known many humans and didn't pay much attention to individuals. I wondered if he knew that Misty was about to retire and was counting the days until the same fate would overtake him.

Norah was fussing over Annie in the yard beside us. As calm as was Cappie, Annie was nervy. She moved around, swinging her head this way and that, her ears swivelling at all the new sounds in this unknown environment.

"Sweet, sweet baby," said Norah in a soothing sing-song voice. "Tomorrow, we'll fly around that course, and your hoofs will barely touch the ground. You're such a good girl. You know that I love you."

We hunkered down in the truck that night. Mrs Heyward, Norah and I slept on mattresses in the area above the truck cabin. We opened all the windows so that there was a cool breeze flowing through otherwise the heat would have been stifling.

Chapter Eight – Take Your Own Line

I woke early, slid down from the raised area above the cabin of the truck where I had slept with Norah and Mrs Heyward, tip-toed across to the ramp and descended. The morning air was fresh, and the world looked like it had just washed its face. I set to preparing breakfast. We had a gas stove to heat a kettle of water for tea and coffee. There was a metal contraption into which one put a slice of bread to toast over the flame. There were bottles of milk, water, and jam in a cool box with a big block of ice. John was up and went off to feed the horses and fill their water buckets.

The first jumping competition was for novice horses. And then there was a high jump, which John told me was very popular with the crowd. He was completely mad about this particular competition and had been practising excessively. "It's built specially with a baulk board that stands about 4 feet 6 inches, and thick four-inch rails rise above that. There are giant wings higher than the jump, which sort of frames it and encourages the horses to jump."

The height was four feet six in the first round, then it would go up to five feet, five six, and then increase by increments of four inches. I found this focus on jumping massive heights somewhat off-putting. I thought the exercise of flowing around a course was a more genuine test of horsemanship and skills. The Heywards didn't share my reservations. This was perfectly normal for them. Everyone was entered.

John told me how, in 1946, Jack Martin was riding a horse called Gold Meade, and they set a record of 8 feet 6 inches.

"Isn't it rather hard on the horses' legs?" I asked sceptically.

"They bury hundreds of old motor car tyres under the take-off side of the jump, and they land in sawdust."

"I suppose that has a trampoline effect," I replied thoughtfully.

Cappie was feeling fresh and invigorated. I think he knew that this was the real thing, not just more training, which was a waste of time for him. I wore my best pair of cream jodhpurs and a dark blue riding jacket. My long black leather boots were so shiny they were dazzling. I felt it was good luck to dress my best. About half a dozen riders and horses were thundering around the area where a practice jump was set up at five feet. After trotting and cantering circles for thirty minutes, I waited my turn for the practice jump. Cappie bounced over, tucking his feet up. I felt hopeful. I wasn't even going to ask how high Cappie had ever jumped. I thought I should try my best and see how high we could go.

More and more riders and horses congregated in the collecting ring, and an endless stream of horses and riders leapt over the practice jump, which now stood at five feet six. Robbie put Hussy over the jump at least half a dozen times. John didn't bother to go over the practice jump. He was lounging in the saddle, one leg cocked over the pommel, chatting away with other riders catching up with the show circuit gossip. Norah took Annie to a quiet side of the showground and walked her around on a long rein. Mrs Heyward rode with her on Dunker. She was all dressed up in a show jacket of dusty grey with a black velvet collar. It was gathered in the modern fashion at the waist with a stylish flair draping over the saddle's cantle.

"Hi," said a girl riding a dapple-grey lanky thoroughbred. "That is Cappie, isn't it? The Heywards' horse?"

"Yes, that's right. They've kindly asked me to ride him this summer. My name is Jill. I'm from England," I replied.

"I'm Ellie Cosgrove," she said. "You lot are coming out to stay at our place after the show."

"How do you do?" I said formally, conscious that I hadn't picked up the Australian relaxed communication style yet.

"Oh! You sound so terribly English," she cried, cackling like a demented hen.

'Why is that funny?' I thought but gave her a smile that did not reach my eyes.

"How do you like old Cappie?" she asked. "You know he used to be my horse before the Heywards took him on. We did all things Pony Club for years. He's such a reliable old soldier."

"He's good to ride," I said stiffly, still not unbending after she had laughed at my British accent. "Today, this event will be my first time going to a competition with him."

"He's brilliant at the high jump," she said.

"Then, if something goes wrong, it will be down to me," I replied.

"There's nothing for certain in the showjumping game. That's why I like it!"

"What's your horse like?" I asked, looking over her mount. I didn't want to be too critical, but he seemed seriously underweight.

"He's a windsucker," she explained, "if you're wondering why he's so thin. We've tried everything, but we just can't cure him."

Windsucking is when the horse bites into something and sucks in air which fills his stomach and makes him disinclined to eat.

"That's unfortunate," I said.

"Looks like the event is about to start. Must just canter a few circles. I'm third to go. I hate waiting around best to get it over and done with. You better make sure you're ready to go. They trundle us through pretty quickly, just one jump each and then the next."

I trotted old Cappie around. He was very calm. I rode him over the practice jump once more. I watched Ellie jump her grey thoroughbred, and they cleared the rails easily.

"Well done," I called as she left the arena.

Norah came up.

"You ready to go, Jill?" she asked. I think it's two more, and then you and me."

"How is Annie going today?" I asked.

"A bit edgy, but that's normal for her and me," she said ruefully.

I watched her ride in, circle around, and then head for the jump. Annie seemed to half-shy a few strides before, and she took off too early, hitting the top pole with her hind hoofs. Norah gave her a big pat.

"Bad luck," I called and pushed Cappie into a trot, presenting myself to the steward, who ticked my name off the list. I cantered half a circle and then turned towards the jump. Cappie approached steadily and picked his take-off point, and I went along with him. We cleared the jump easily, and I felt hugely relieved. I would have hated to have failed at the first obstacle. I had something to prove.

Robbie galloped past me into the ring, turning Pepperpot on his haunches. He gave him a short run-off and leapt over the jump.

'Show off,' I thought to myself.

John was next with Hussy, and they cantered a steady circle before he set her at the jump. He was workmanlike and proficient in how he rode, and they cleared the top bar easily. So, four became three. The class had about thirty entrants, and there were twenty in the second round. The rails were raised six inches to five feet.

I refused to be daunted, and when they called my number, I cantered into the ring. Again, Cappie flew over and cleared the rail. Robbie and Pepperpot went clear, and so did John. Now, it was down to twelve contestants. The top rail was carefully measured at five feet six inches. It was getting serious. I don't think I had ever jumped higher than this, so if we went clear, I would have to jump higher than I had ever done before.

Cappie wasn't fazed, and he easily cleared the top rail. John and Pepperpot did the usual flourishing leap, but this time, they misjudged the height and a trailing hind hoof brought down the top rail.

"Idiot," remonstrated John as he cantered in. His judgmental attitude didn't bring him good luck. He rode Hussy competently and sensibly, but still, she didn't clear the top rail. Now, I was the only representative of the Heywards' stable. The rail was raised to five feet ten, and only six of us were left. Cappie was a total star and took me over clear. It would be six feet two inches in the next round. I was starting to get properly nervous.

I walked around the collecting ring, wanting to stay quiet to prepare myself. Cappie didn't take any notice of my nervousness. I saw John striding over towards us. I halted and waited for his approach.

"You know you just have to leave it to him," he said in a lecturing tone.

That was the first thing I had learned about riding Cappie and I resented him trying to tell me how to ride the horse.

"Yes," I replied.

They were calling us in, and I rode Cappie forward. It would be the highest I had ever jumped if we cleared six feet two. We cantered a wide circle, and then we turned, and I sat tight, pushing with my legs on every stride. He took off from right under the jump and catapulted into the air. It reminded me a little of how Rapide jumped when I first had him. I looked down when we were in mid-air, and the rail below us stayed put. We were over, and we had gone clear.

Three of us went clear, and three were out. Those three would jump off again for fourth place, but first, we had to find a winner. Six feet six inches seemed just too high, and I wasn't sure I could make it. I even considered withdrawing from the competition, but I couldn't do that. My pride wouldn't let me. I had to forge on. The worst that could happen was that we would bring down the rail, and that was what we did. Cappie just tipped it, and it fell.

The two remaining riders, tough-looking men on tall thoroughbreds, went clear and then it was up to six feet 10. One cleared it, the other didn't. So, we had first, second, and I was third. It was a creditable result, and I felt chuffed. I rode in for the yellow ribbon and an envelope with our winnings.

"You're brilliant old chap," I murmured to Cappie as we cantered around the arena.

"That's not a bad result at all," said Mrs Heyward, giving me a wide congratulatory smile.

The Heyward children all clapped me on the back and said, 'well done'. I felt intensely relieved. I had proved myself, and now I could relax and enjoy the rest of the competitions. I had jumped higher than ever before.

For lunch, Mrs Heyward brought us all the hamburgers in Aussie style. I had never tasted such a combination: meat burgers with salad and a fried egg, cheese, beetroot and pineapple rings. It was an unusual mixture but quite delicious, and I wondered whether we shouldn't put them on the menu at Blainstock Castle for the paying guests, with lamingtons for dessert.

After lunch was a Take Your Own Line event. You had to take all the jumps in any order you chose. As soon as the course was arranged, we got in a huddle and started drawing designs on pieces of paper. There were heated disputes between Robbie and John. Of course, with his ability to turn on his haunches, spurts of speed and agility, Pepperpot gave Robbie the advantage. John believed that with a superior strategy, anyone could succeed. Norah walked into the ring and floated around, imagining herself to be Annie and presumably came up with a plan, or perhaps she was going to drift around incorporating Annie's nervous shies and veers in any direction. I sat and puzzled over my diagram. I was somewhat visually-spatially challenged. Words were my master skill. I asked John his plan, but he kept it close to his chest.

Cappie was dozing quietly in his stall. He was an old hand and knew he should relax when offered the opportunity. Annie was more nervous than ever. She was turning circles to the left incessantly. Norah went over and put on her head collar, sat on an upturned bucket and gently stroked her, murmuring words of comfort. When it came to her mare, she was endlessly patient and understanding.

I had devised a course which I felt was do-able. This was going to be a fascinating event to watch. I was due to jump tenth so I would be able to see what the nine riders before me did. John was after me, then Robbie, then Norah. I cantered a few circles to warm up Cappie and then kept him walking. He was his usual calm self, and I began to appreciate his equable temperament. He was the perfect schoolmaster for me in this alien environment. I was stretching my boundaries, coping with these new challenges.

Each of the competitors before me jumped a different pattern. The first was a weather-beaten man, his brown face laced with lines from the harsh sun, a limp and ragged moustache drooping over his mouth. The loudspeaker announced that he was Billie Tennant from Charleville. Robbie explained that this was a town in the far west of Queensland. With his eyes narrowed against the glaring sunlight, Billie jumped around the outside, jumps in a wide curve, then wove his way between the obstacles in the centre, galloping with a flourish over the finishing line. He had gone clear, and his time was fast. I could see that this would be a hard-fought competition.

The second and third riders were zig-zagging here and there, and it was hard to discern their strategy. One had two jumps down, and the other's horse refused when he came in at an impossible angle to a wide triple. The horse knew that he would never make it and ducked out. I decided to stick to my plan and mentally jumped each jump, envisaging the approach and then remembering whether it was straight on, turn left, or right on landing.

They called my number, and I cantered into the ring on Cappie. I felt a rush of pure joy, such as perhaps only a showjumper on a good horse feels at the prospect of an exhilarating round ahead of them. It flashed through my mind, 'this was the life, jumping my way around the world, meeting all sorts of fascinating and strange people along the way.'

I rode over, bowed to the judges in the box on stilts that overlooked the ring, and then cantered on in a wide arc, listening for the bell. Cappie gave a little shake of his head as if telling me that he had this under control. We wove through my plan of jumps. I ensured that we had at least three strides before each jump to come in straight and true, and Cappie obliged by clearing every rail. I knew it wouldn't be the fastest time, but we went clear and had not disgraced ourselves.

As we left the ring, John passed me, his mouth set in a determined line, riding with a firmness that I suspected a temperamental chestnut mare like Hussy needed to keep her on track. I hoped they would do well. It seemed to matter so much to John that he did well. He was the opposite of his happy-go-lucky brother. I dismounted and loosened Cappie's girth and watched from the ringside. I had to admit he had chosen a clever line, better than my own design, and he was pushing Hussy hard to gain speed between every jump, with precision turns and clever angles. He was clear and fast but a few seconds slower than that first rider from the outback, Billie Tennant.

Robbie followed him, galloping into the ring on the clever, agile little Pepperpot. He made a dramatic bow to the judge and then waved to the crowd, who cheered him. He was such a showman with his wide grin and exhibitionist tendencies. As could have been predicted, he took the most daring of lines, turning on the spot and giving his brave Pepperpot only one stride before he had to make prodigious leaps at impossible angles. Miraculously, against any sensible prediction, they went clear and two seconds faster than Billie Tennant. The crowd cheered vigorously, and the pair galloped out of the ring. I sighed. This was going to upset John for sure.

Norah was next, and she and Annie also went clear, but their time was not fast and she was out of the running. At that moment, I was standing fourth, but I doubted that I would stay there. There were another fifteen competitors to go. I rode back to the truck and tied Cappie to the rail with a bucket of water and a hay net. I untacked him, gave him a good rub down, and then threw a fly rug over him. He was such a wise and clever old fellow. He deserved the best of my attention.

Mrs Heyward made me a mug of tea, and I relaxed in one of the comfortable chairs and munched into a huge lamington. I decided that this was a pretty decent life. One could really settle into this Antipodean experience. I forgot that I would meet my father in less than a week. I had been lying awake at night worrying about this since arriving in Australia, but the excitement of competing had put it out of my mind.

The results of the Take Your Own Line were being announced. Robbie was the winner, followed by Billie Tennant, but John hadn't come anywhere. I knew that this was going to upset him. Then, I remembered Mrs Darcy's strictures on being a good loser and caring about the horse and standards of horsemanship. I didn't think it would be a good idea to try and pass on any of these ideas when John rode back to camp, his face like thunder. It was no use hoping that Robbie wouldn't be gloating and boasting all evening, and this would just make it worse.

Mrs Heyward had been into the butcher's and came back with some enormous rump steaks, thick and juicy. She prepared onions, mushrooms, tomatoes and boiled potatoes and we ate a hearty feast, followed by mugs of tea and apple tart with thick cream.

"Got to keep your strength up," she said, ignoring the tension between her sons. "Tomorrow is the Table A competition, and also the pairs. Have you thought who might go with whom?"

You could have cut the tension with a knife. No one would choose to go with Norah, who was the least competitive of us. I didn't mind at all; I just wanted a fair resolution of the issue.

"I'm pairing up with Ellie Cosgrove," said Robbie. Her father is bringing over her other horse tonight and we should be in with a good chance.

"I thought Jill and Cappie could be with me and Hussy," said John.

"I thought I would give Annie a rest tomorrow," said Norah. "She's been brilliant today. Also, there's an art gallery in town with an exhibition by a Sydney painter who I actually met one night when I was out with Michael."

"That's a good idea," said Mrs Heyward. "I think I might come with you. I want to look around for some gifts for the Cosgroves. We don't want to turn up empty-handed."

Thus, the plan was set. I could only hope Cappie and I would acquit ourselves well and not rouse John's ire.

That night, we slept soundly, dead to the world. The exertion of the day's competitions had taken it out of us, and there was more to come tomorrow.

Chapter Nine – Cappie's Trick

On the second day of the show, I woke early. My body was still at odds with the new time zone and I lit the gas stove and prepared mugs with milk and sugar and put loose-leaf black tea in the old brown teapot. John crawled out of his swag, gulped down a mug of tea and went over to feed the horses and clean out the yards. He had a tendency to black-edged anger and humourlessness, but he was a worker and always the first to do the mundane tasks. Robbie slept on. Soon Mrs Heyward emerged fully dressed in crisp white shirt and an elegantly cut skirt and brogues. It seemed that her turnout was flawless no matter whether we were camping, or she was at home with her walk-in wardrobe. The sun was low on the horizon but already I could feel the heat of the day shimmering in the distance. There hadn't been one drop of rain since I had arrived. Magpies were carking in the gum trees that ringed the showground and a flock of pink and white galahs flew overhead.

"The Table A competition begins at ten this morning, I'll have to drag that sleepyhead Robbie out of his swag," says Mrs Heyward, delicately sipping her tea which she took without milk or sugar. "What did you think of the jumping yesterday, Jill?"

"I really enjoyed it," I replied enthusiastically. "I'm thinking that I should institute the Take Your Own Line in Oxfordshire. I thought I would write to my friend Ann and explain it to her, and she can get in touch with the organisers of our local show at Chatton. If we could get some decent prizes from the local community then they may come from far and wide. Such a top idea!"

Norah floated down in a gypsy dress, rubbing her eyes. Her thick cloud of dark hair was a mass of curls around her sweet face. She was different from the girl I had met in Scotland when she had been a schoolgirl on holiday with her parents. She was developing her own style. I wondered whether the relationship with her poet was going to end in tears. As charming and exotic as he was, he didn't seem like the settling down type.

I sat there with my mug of tea and my mind wandered off. I was musing over the idea that a woman might have a different life than finding 'the one' and settling down to have children. Our world was changing, and a lot of the entrenched post-war ideas were being tipped on their head. Ann followed the traditional course with her upcoming marriage to the estimable Henry, who would undoubtedly make a good husband. I had hoped that I might follow the same course with Frank Stabley, which would entail being a farmer's wife and producing a brood of children who would provide a lot of useful help during the busy harvest season. I had always imagined that I would like to have my own farm, somewhere like where my ponies had stayed at Mrs York's place when Ann and I had helped her organise some autumn horse events. There had been stalls with red brick floors set out in herringbone patterns, a barn filled with hay and straw and a harness room for tack. Then the thought occurred to me that there would be no more gallivanting around the world, having horsey adventures wherever I went, meeting all sorts of weird and fascinating people. I would have to settle down. I suddenly wondered whether a farmer's wife might have to spend a lot of time cooking meals for her family and any farm workers, as well as managing hens, collecting eggs, tending a vegetable garden, attending local community events and probably doing things like the flowers in the local church.

This thought was a trifle depressing. Not to mention that although Frank had hinted at his interest in me, he had not come close to declaring his undying passion. Perhaps he would decide that I was not 'the one'. The thought occurred to me that I might end up being an old maid. Ann and Henry, Mercedes and Mark, Susan and Barty, even Clarissa and her old husband, April and the wandering-eyed Gary were all paired up, and I had only vague hopes of Frank. Mummy had tentatively suggested that it was because I hadn't grown up with a father, and this was a very disturbing thought. But even more disturbing was going to be meeting the man who I had thought was dead throughout my whole childhood. But I had to concentrate on showjumping today. Partnering with John and Hussy in the Pairs competition would be daunting.

Then a random thought struck me, as such things do when the really serious issues of life rear their gruesome heads. It was thinking about Mrs York and the farm where Black Boy and Rapide had been kept during our sojourn at Pockett House. Cecilia, my cousin, was the daughter of Mummy's sister Primrose. Did Aunt Primrose know the dreaded secret that my father had been in prison for manslaughter? I hadn't thought to quiz Mummy about just who else might know about this. Did Cecilia know? Surely not. She would have spilt the beans for sure.

"Penny, for your thoughts," said Robbie, giving me a knowing look. "Dreaming of your boyfriend?"

"Ha Ha!" I replied in a jocular manner. It was time to think about the day's showjumping competition. The Table A was the standard format in which I had competed since my first gymkhana on Black Boy. All the competitors trooped in to walk the course. Technically, one is meant to be dressed in full kit for this phase, but it was obviously more relaxed here. Riders were in their shirtsleeves, not wearing their hard hats nor slapping crops against their boots. There was a lot of jolly banter, and although some riders were seriously stepping it out to count the paces between different elements and walking the line between related fences, there were also those who seemed to drift around gossiping about the events of the previous evening when there had been a party at the other end of the showground.

The course was well designed. I couldn't fault the sturdy jumps with their decent cups that meant that poles wouldn't fall in a puff of wind. The pacing between the elements was spot on. The jumps were gaily painted green, blue, white, red and orange. I wondered at the hardness of the ground that would not be easy on the horses' legs.

"We'll have to screw in those studs for dry ground," said John, who was walking beside me. He seemed to have decided that I was up to snuff, and we discussed the various angles and approaches. The happy-go-lucky Robbie was surrounded by a crowd of young women who were vying for his attention.

We went back to the truck and tightened the horses' girths. John busied himself screwing in thick rounded studs which would give the horses' purchase on the dry ground, and then we mounted, ready for the warmup. We were early in the competition as we had been the day before and would not have many competitors to watch before we had to jump.

I trotted and cantered a few circles and then walked Cappie. He didn't need to settle down, as he was such an old hand at this game. I was as nervous and tense as a bushranger in his first bail-up as I watched Billy Tennant, the rider from Charleville go first. He went fast and clear, and I knew the competition would be stiff. I was determined to prove my worth, and Cappie rose to the occasion, albeit in a casual Australian way. He zipped around, clearing each fence, turning at the merest touch of the rein. He did feel a little long in the stride, and he took off before I would have judged it, but he cleared the fences, so I left him to it. Robbie went clear, but unfortunately for John, Hussy was not in the mood, and she seemed to almost deliberately knock down four jumps. I felt sorry for him. I knew that he was going to take this to heart. I dreaded having to ride with him in the pairs competition this afternoon. He rode up to me as he came out of the ring.

"She's in season and not at all cooperative today," he said. I thought that she was never cooperative, but I just nodded in agreement. "I think I should ride Annie in the pairs with you this afternoon."

"Really!" I exclaimed, surprised. "But isn't she Norah's horse?"

"We don't mind swapping around sometimes. The partnerships are not set in stone. I rode her in several competitions when Norah was away in Tasmania, and Hussy was out of action. She and I get on alright. Also, the good point is that she is really fond of Cappie, and they can stick like glue together as they jump. You get points for style, and those two are like twins."

"That sounds good," I said, thinking that Annie, neurotic as she might be, was unlikely to kick us as we went around the ring.

Robbie and I had been waiting for ages for the jump-off. As usual, he was surrounded by young women, including Ellie Cosgrove, who was riding a very scruffy-looking flea-bitten grey, only 14.2 hh.

"Robbie said this was your Pony Club mount," I commented to her.

"Yes, he's still my favourite, no matter how many bigger horses I ride."

She said this so casually that I imagined she had squillions of riding horses to choose from, the paddocks of their big farm teeming with rideable horses.

The jump-off would sort us out and there probably wouldn't be many more clear rounds. The jumps were well over five feet, and there were some very tricky twists and turns if you chose the quickest path between the obstacles. I sat there mentally, riding the way I was going to go. I had decided to push Cappie to his limits and insist on a bit more collection so he could turn on his haunches and take off with only one or two strides on each approach. The gate, perhaps the flimsiest of all the jumps, was the one I would take at an angle. I was feeling a bit dare-devilish. If I didn't take risks, we would come nowhere, especially competing against clever little ponies like those of Robbie and Ellie.

I was called and rode into the ring brim full of determination. Cappie seemed to sense my attitude and shook his head vigorously. I exerted my will, took a tighter feel on the reins, and applied my legs. Remember that cry 'Legs, legs, legs!' that had been the mantra of my youth. Cappie spun on his hindquarters so sharply that I lurched and then came the slanting approach to the gate, and we were up and over. Our time was fast, even a fraction of a second faster than Billie Tennant.

Robbie must have been determined to beat us and followed the same path that I had chosen. He took the gate almost sideways and came to grief. It fell in a heap, which seemed to jinx the rest of his round, and three more jumps fell. He was grinning ruefully when he rode out. He really didn't seem to care. It was all just fun for him.

Eventually, there were six clear rounds, and they called us in order of the shortest times. I was amazed that I was second, with Billie Tennant third.

Ellie Cosgrove had won with a whole two seconds faster than me. I felt very pleased with Cappie as we cantered around the ring with our ribbon tied around the neck and the envelope of cash winnings clutched in one hand. I felt as if I were not letting the side down.

'Well done!' said John, perhaps a little more robustly than needed. He was determined to be sporting and a good loser. My respect for him increased. He might seem a little stodgy, but he was a good egg. Robbie grinned at me and slapped me on the back. The three of us ate the sandwiches Mrs Heyward made for us this morning before she and Norah went into town. Then, we wandered into the area with food stalls, a few showground rides, a small merry-go-round for younger children, and some swirling teacups.

"Have you tried a dagwood dog yet?" asked Robbie.

"They're disgusting. A sausage deep fried several times in batter on a stick" chipped in John.

"I must admit they don't look very appetising," I said. "I'll think I'll give it a miss."

"Come on, let's go back. I got Mum to get me a big bag of ice. I want to sponge down the horses' legs with icy water to stop them from getting swollen with this hard ground. Especially Cappie, I noticed this morning that his tendons were a little filled," said John.

It was a good idea. I wasn't used to hard ground. Most of the time, the ground in England was too soft and muddy. The other problem was the flies bothering the horses. We sprayed them with fly spray several times daily, covering their eyes with cupped hands.

"I could do with a bit of this icy water myself," I said, splashing my face and turning to face the breeze. I didn't think I would ever get used to this heat. The dust and the flies made it even harder to bear.

I heard them calling for competitors to walk the course for the Pairs Competition. We strolled over. John was, predictably, very serious. We discussed every approach, every stride, corner and our pace. As Annie tended to shy or turn to the left when she was nervous we decided that Cappie would ride on the left, with her on the right. Robbie and Ellie were capering around, pretending to buck and shy, propping and rushing forward like a couple of wild horses. They reminded me of the kids involved in events I had organised who were always clowning around, acting the fool. Such people used to drive me nuts, but now that I was older, I could appreciate their light-hearted approach to life.

"We used to call them the Terrible Twins when they were younger," said John. "Sometimes, we would spend the whole summer at the Cosgroves' property when Mum and Dad went on one of their European trips. Robbie and Ellie were always up to mischief, the bane of the gardener's life. He was called Diggles, and we all laughed behind his back at his funny name. They would play ridiculous pranks on him, and he would storm around threatening to cut their heads off with an old-fashioned scythe. They were ragging everyone, and besides Diggles, I usually got the worst of it.

"They do look like twins as well," I replied. "Ellie is tall and dark like all you Heywards. It will be fab to go to the Cosgroves' property. I've never been on a farm so big. We've got quite a few acres up in Scotland, but it's mainly moorland that is not really used for stock. There are some sheep, but there is more wildlife like deer and grouse."

"Check out the course," said John, changing the subject.

I turned my attention to what was happening in the ring. The course for this competition was different. The jumps had been widened so that two horses could jump side by side. They were not as high as the Table A had been this morning. The first round had a generous time limit, and those who went clear went on to a jump-off when the jumps were raised a few inches, and three judges were scoring us for keeping together and being in sync.

I was nervous about partnering with John. He took everything to heart, and I didn't want to let him down. We cantered together around the practice area. As usual, Annie was glued to Cappie's side when they went side by side. We sailed over the practice jumps in perfect synchrony.

"I think we're in with a real chance. I should have thought of riding Annie in the first place," said John.

We were called and cantered in to salute the judge. I flashed my best smile, and off we went. The bell rang, and we were through the start. The first jump was a simple straight fence, and we rode over together. Annie's long stride exactly matched Cappie's, and it was simply a matter of steering them. When we turned to the right to face the wide triple, I lengthened Cappie's stride, and when we turned to the left, I shortened him up while John pushed Annie on. We had just two jumps to go, and Cappie vigorously shook his head. To my shock, I saw the headpiece slipping over his ears, and I was holding the reins while the bridle was flapping loose below his neck.

John saw what had happened.

"Stay close and keep going," he commanded.

I didn't have much choice. There was no chance to pull up.

John steered Annie towards a plank fence, and I used my legs vigorously to keep Cappie next to her. They jumped perfectly. I was truly a passenger.

Then we had to swing to the left, and John rode Annie in such a way that she was shouldering Cappie like a professional polo pony.

We were still side by side, and over we went and headed for the last fence, a formidable hogsback. I sat tight, and we swept towards it. Cappie put on a spurt of speed, so John had to push Annie on to keep pace with him. They rose together, and we were perfectly placed side by side. Then we galloped with a flourish through the finish. Cappie kept on going, and we zoomed through the exit gate and towards the truck. He realised I had no control, and he wanted his haynet. He slid to a stop, and I toppled off, landing on my feet breathless with the effort of riding with no bridle. John came trotting up behind me. He was grinning.

"I forgot about that trick of Cappie's!" he said.

"That's a bonza horse!" shouted a rider who was going by, presumably referring to Cappie.

"You forgot! You didn't think to warn me!" I exclaimed.

"Well, we kept together, didn't we? What's the problem?"

"What's to stop him doing it again?" I asked.

"I'll see if we've got an extended throat latch headpiece in the bottom of the trunk. We used to ride him in it, but I guess somehow he got put back into a regular bridle."

"Brilliant!" I said. "If we can't find one, we can buy one at the tack shop in Bowral, but not in time for the jump-off. I don't want to ride him again and have that happen."

Robbie and Ellie rode over to the truck, laughing conspiratorially together.

"How did you go?" I asked.

"We went clear, but Ellie's pony seemed to think it was a race, so we didn't stay together very well. Not like you two," replied Robbie.

So, we were all in the jump-off. John had miraculously found a bridle with an extended throat latch. I hadn't seen one of these before. Usually, the headpiece and throat latch were part of one piece of leather threading through the browband loops. This one had a browband with two leather loops on each side. One for the cheek straps and the outer one for a separate throat latch, which included its own piece of leather that went over the top of the poll. Hastily, I rubbed some saddle soap on it, and then we put it together to fit Cappie's head. I imagined that he was looking rather proud of his bad behaviour. He knew exactly what he had done.

They called for competitors who had gone clear, and we heard our numbers.

"Let's go!" said Robbie, mounting Pepperpot, his long legs hanging below the pony's stomach. We cantered in a foursome to the collecting ring. There were half a dozen other pairs, including Billie Tennant, partnered with a skinny young man on an equally thin weedy-type of thoroughbred.

"That's his nephew," whispered Ellie. "Some people have said that they're unbeatable."

"Well, perhaps 'some people' are wrong," retorted John. We grinned at each other. We were both confident but didn't want to tempt fate with brave assertions of our ability.

We were to go first, so at least we didn't have to wait around. We set off together, and it was one of those rounds that stood out in my memory when absolutely nothing went wrong. Cappie must have felt that he had to make up for his behaviour in the first round, and he communicated this to Annie, who didn't engage in any silly nervous shenanigans.

We went clear and fast, and both of us grinned widely. Spectators clapped from the ringside, and it was a wonderful moment. I was sure we would get top marks for style if the rather weird-looking extended throat latch didn't detract from our appearance. Robbie and Ellie went well together, and she managed to rein in her pony, so they more or less kept pace side by side. Then, there was Billie Tennant and his young relative. They set off at a tremendous pace, but the young man's horse swerved away from the penultimate plank fence, which meant they were out of the running. There were two more clear rounds, but John and I were first when the winners were announced, and Robbie and Ellie were second.

"This is a grand day for the Heywards, Cosgroves and Crewes!" said Mrs Heyward, who was standing watching at the ringside with Norah after having just returned from their shopping trip.

"Aren't we clever?" I said happily. I was pleased that I had acquitted myself well. I would have hated to have my head in the dust.

"Yes, you are all wonderfully brilliant," she replied.

Norah was dancing around with excitement. She was hugging a small brown flat parcel to her chest.

"What is that you've got?" I asked.

"It's a painting by Michael's friend. I had to show solidarity, and I believe one day, it will be worth a fortune when dear Ricky becomes famous. And I've got a present for you, Jill."

"But it's not my birthday or anything," I said.

"I know, but there was a copy of Michael's latest volume of poems in the bookshop, so I bought it. I'll give it to you now, but when we return to Sydney, you'll have to get him to sign it."

"Thank you very much," I said politely. It would be interesting to read Michael's poems and see whether I thought he had real talent or whether it was merely Norah's hero worship.

We had a celebration dinner that night with two bottles of white fizzy wine that had been put in the coolbox with a block of ice and a lemon mousse cake from the bakery.

"To all of us!" said Robbie, raising his mug of wine.

"To all of us!" we chorused, raising our mugs in unison.

"Jill, why don't you read out some of Michael's poems," suggested Norah mischievously.

I could hardly refuse and began with the first one. Silence fell upon our group, and everyone listened intently as I stumbled over the lines.

"That really is very good poetry," said Ellie.

"That's Norah's love of her life," said Robbie teasingly.

"Don't be silly. He's just a special friend," said Mrs Heyward, a small frown creasing her forehead. "I always thought you might end up with that nice young man who took you to the golf club dance last year. What was his name? Clark, I think."

"Clingy Clark, he just wouldn't flush," said Norah, smiling and giggling as she gulped down more than her share of the bubbly.

The next day, after packing up the truck, eating a leisurely lunch and loading the horses, we set off in convoy following the Cosgroves' fancy horse truck. We had hung our ribbons around the rear vision mirror on the windscreen, and they flapped gaily in the breeze that gusted in through the open windows. Secretly, I was pleased that I had won more ribbons than any of the Heywards or Ellie Cosgrove. Now don't think I had become one of those dastardly pothunters but I felt as if I was on show for my country.

The drive was scenic. For many miles, rows of poplars lined the road. Heat waves rose from the tarmac, shimmering in dancing lines. Windmills stood on metal structures, and John explained that they pumped brackish bore water from deep beneath the earth. There were also groves of wattle trees, acacias bursting with bright yellow buds with dusty olive-green leaves. The very difference between the countryside and the leafy green lanes of Oxfordshire and the heathery moorland of Scotland enthralled me.

The property, called Dunslains, was near Goulburn, the wool dealing hub of New South Wales. They said Australia was riding on the sheep's back, and Australian merino wool was shipped worldwide. We drove past a large elegantly designed brick building, two-stories, with extensive grounds, bounded by high metal fences.

"That's Kenmore Asylum, for the lunatics," said Robbie. "It's famous for being the most haunted building in Australia. Forty years ago, a man murdered his wife there. And the year before there was a pneumonia epidemic and nineteen patients died."

"Really, Robbie, it's for people with psychiatric problems," corrected his mother.

Shortly afterwards, we arrived at the property, turning in through an impressive gateway with a grid, which prevented the animals from walking out. The avenue to the house was at least two miles long and lined with gum trees. Huge open golden paddocks spread beyond the driveway, scorched by the hot summer sun. The house was low set, only one storey, but extremely large and surrounded by a wrap-around verandah. Pendulous purple wisteria twined around posts and hung from the beams above the verandah. Spread out around the house was an extraordinary garden, gracious lawns, arboured walkways, giant oak trees and cunningly placed patches of English garden plants, flowering in every colour of the rainbow, even this late in the summer.

We drove around the back and across a small paddock to the stables almost as splendid as the house. The horses stepped down the ramp, snuffed the dusty air and followed us to their respective stables.

"They've been here before," I observed.

"Yes, we've spent many holidays here. We consider it our second home."

A couple of men unloaded our tack and horse feed, and all the gear was taken to a room allocated to us. John, Robbie, Norah and I took our suitcases and followed a track to the house. It led us around the back, where large galvanised iron water tanks collected rain that fell upon the roof. There was a tree, which John told me was a blackwood, which sounded like a music box. Birdsong poured from it: finches, blue wrens and wagtails. As we trooped through the back garden, a flight of pink and grey galahs rose, squawking from the high branches of a tall, white gum. Three wedge-tailed eagles soared overhead.

I began to get a grasp on the Cosgroves. They were a colonial family born into privilege and tradition, part of the squattocracy. Squatters were the farmers of extensive landholdings where they had moved in and tamed the land many years ago when white Europeans first settled in Australia. The Cosgroves were at the top of the rural establishment. Dunslains was not just a farm. It was a rural fiefdom, a vast pastoral holding. The inside of the house was something else. There were high, ornate ceilings trimmed with intricate cornices and plaster roses. All the floors were polished cedar wood scattered with many costly hand-made Persian rugs.

Ellie gave us a quick tour of the house and it was the library that impressed me most. It was a large, oak-panelled room furnished with studded armchairs. There was a masculine air to this room, as if it was the place where the men in the family and local notables would meet and make important decisions about pastoral matters and local and national politics. A grandfather clock stood tall between shelves of leather-bound books, ticking loudly. There was a Chesterfield settee that faced the sandstone fireplace. The solid, traditional furniture and dark colours spoke of power. I remembered John's description of the wealth of the Cosgroves who ruled the land which spread for miles around their splendid country home.

I was sharing a large bedroom with Norah. Two single beds were placed in the middle of the room. Long windows looked over the home paddock with its splendid collection of gum trees. An arrangement of gum tips and freesias on the dressing table was quite an unusual and imaginative combination.

After unpacking and lying on our beds to rest, we put on our best dresses, brushed our hair, went down to dinner and met the rest of the family. Only Ellie and one of the employees had attended the show at Bowral. Now we met Mr and Mrs and the two other adult children. Mr Cosgrove was a traditional squatter dressed in white moleskins, a checked shirt and a plain tie. He was a handsome man with a large, square body — an imposing figure. Mrs Cosgrove was elegant and well-spoken, wearing an extremely well-cut frock that flowed around her willowy figure. Another daughter, Priscilla, was a carbon copy of her mother, not a tomboy like her sister Ellie. She was devoted to the local community and was engaged to a young farmer of the same ilk as her family. The son was very like a younger version of his father. He was extraordinarily handsome and well-spoken, and he studied law at a university in Sydney. They said he was destined to be a politician and perhaps Prime Minister. He would also inherit the pastoral company. What a catch he would be! There had been hopes that he and Norah might marry, but although they were good friends, there was no romantic spark. I couldn't help but wonder whether I might catch his eye. The idea of marrying into this family was not unpleasant. I felt a pang of guilt about Frank Stabley, but no young woman could have helped but notice Alisdair Cosgrove. I beamed at him and tried a vague coquettish bat of my eyelids. He was very polite, but he didn't pay me any more attention than he paid to anyone else.

I followed the others to the dining room for our evening meal. We passed by the ballroom. Dinner conversation consisted of the events at the show at Bowral, followed by some talk about the current activities at Dunslains. It had been a good year, and the wool clip had been most satisfactory. A mob of bullocks had sold at good prices at the local sales, and all the haysheds were fast filling with good-sized bales.

Alisdair was due back at university soon. Ellie was also off to university. She had finished school the year before and was to do a Bachelor of Arts majoring in English literature. She was fascinated when John mentioned that I wrote books, but I was quick to assure her that my pony books were not exactly high literature, but what I hoped was a 'jolly good read'.

After dinner, we went out into the garden. There were still several hours before it would get dark, and Mrs Cosgrove took us around proudly displaying her plants. I tried to take an intelligent interest, but gardening had never been my forte. If it had been my cousin, Cecilia, she would have been rapt. She had spent much of her childhood pressing poor, dead flowers between the pages of heavy books. Aunt Primrose had written to Mummy recently and told her how Cecilia was now spending a great deal of time in the garden tending to the herbaceous borders.

While John, Alisdair, Priscilla, Norah, Mrs Heyward, Mrs Cosgrove and I conversed politely, Robbie and Ellie were shinning up a tall spreading oak tree.

"The tree house is up there. It's one of their favourite lairs," explained Mrs Cosgrove.

We admired the two tennis courts flanked by well-tended roses in full bloom. Mrs Cosgrove was in cahoots with the gardener, Diggles, grafting chosen plants and trying to breed a new cultivar.

We're having problems with aphids," she said, but that line of conversation went nowhere as none of us knew anything about the subject of aphids, which were apparently the curse of many rose gardeners.

A gazebo overlooking the tennis courts was a large octagonal structure embellished with fretwork. A vine heavy with orange conical blooms had insinuated itself through the roof frame.

"We can offer our guests croquet as well as tennis," said Mrs Heyward, lifting the lid of one of the box sets in the gazebo.

"Let's go down to the waterhole. I fancy a swim," said Robbie, having descended from the oak tree. He was impatient for more robust activities, obviously not fascinated with the prospect of croquet.

"Certainly, would you like to get your bathers girls?" asked Alisdair.

We dashed up to our bedrooms, got changed, assembled again, and trooped across the home paddock where the stock horses grazed.

"What's that quaint building over there?" I asked.

"It's our chapel," explained Alisdair. "There is a family plot behind it where we all get buried when our time comes. Three generations of the family lie there. You know it's one of the oldest parts of the station. The walls are made of wattle and daub."

"You have your own chapel!" I exclaimed. Not even the Duke and Duchess of Tolkington at Pevensy Park had their own chapel. We came to a billabong, the Australian word for a pond. It was large, edged with tall bullrushes and reeds, with a floating pontoon, a water pump at the edge and a small boat.

"The water flows in from the creek at that end and out there at the other," explained Alisdair. "It means it never gets stagnant unless it is a severe drought."

"Last one in is a .." cried Robbie, his words lost as he splashed noisily into the water. He surfaced and with swift arm movements, struck out for the pontoon. Ellie was close behind him. Tentatively, I walked in from the edge. Below the water was ooey-gooey mud, and I hoped there were no creatures. It seemed safer to plunge into the water and swim than walk around the edge. It was very cool and refreshing. I kept my head up, not wanting my hair to get muddy, and breast stroked out towards the pontoon. Norah swam behind me. Priscilla chose not to swim and sat watching us from her position on a log in the dappled shade of the river gums.

We hauled ourselves up to sit on the pontoon.

"Look at those quacking white ducks!" I exclaimed as a mob of them clustered down one end of the body of water.

"Yes, we have duck at least once a week," said Ellie merrily. "Cook has a variety of sauces, including orange, plum, and cherry. "If you were to stay until tomorrow night, you could have sampled one."

We splashed happily for at least half an hour and then walked back across the paddock to the house. The shadows were long. A half-moon had risen over the horizon as the sun set. The light changed, and the colour of the leaves had turned into tiny pennants of silver. Robbie and Ellie had wandered off, and I saw him pushing her on a swing at the end of the garden.

"Do you think you should get an early night, John and Jill? You've got to be up early to drive down to the mountains," said Mrs Heyward.

This elicited polite and interested enquiries about why we should go to the mountains. I was at a loss. I didn't want to lie, but I didn't feel comfortable talking about my long-lost father, who had gone to prison for murder.

"Jill is visiting a family relative who lives in Corryong," replied Mrs Heyward quickly.

"You'll find the mountains interesting," said Mrs Cosgrove, who sensed that there was more to this story. "I'll make sure that Cook prepares you a hamper so you can picnic along the way."

"That is very kind," I said. "I think I will make tracks to bed. It's been a long day."

I scurried off before there were any more awkward questions. I went to sleep and didn't even wake when Norah came up to bed much later in the evening.

Chapter Eleven– Corryong

We left Dunslains early in the morning as the gentle dawn light spread shadows on the lawns.

"Look! Look!" I cried. There were four silver-grey kangaroos nibbling grass on the edge of the paddock next to the garden. They looked up as they heard me shout, and slowly they jumped away.

"Damn nuisance!" muttered John. "They eat the grass that is meant for the stock."

This casual dismissal of my very first sight of these marsupials flattened my rush of joy and exhilaration. I watched them intently, marvelling at their strange shape and gait.

"How long will it take us to get there?" I asked.

"Probably about five hours," calculated John.

"But that's ten hours of driving for you," I said suddenly, conscious of the effort he was putting into transporting me around the country.

"We're used to driving long distances in Australia," he reassured me. "It's no problem. I haven't been down towards the mountains for years, so it will be interesting for me."

On the drive to Corryong, we passed through towns called Gunning, Oolong, Manton, Yass, Bookham, Jugiong, Coolac, then got to Gundagai where we stopped to eat. It was an early lunch, but as usual, I was starving.

"There is a monument of the 'Dog Who Sat on the Tuckerbox' at Gundagai, well actually five miles from Gundagai. It was put up in the early 1930s at the old family camping ground from the bullock team days. There was an old hotel there known as Lazy Larry's. There was one of the old drivers of Cobb and Co's coaches and men who drove bullock teams living there," said John as we drew to a stop near the monument.

I looked at the statue of the kelpie. He was cute, and I guess it was iconic. If one celebrates the past, then better to remember it with a statue of a noble working dog than some sordid war. John began to recite the poem:

As I was coming down Conroy's Gap
I heard a maiden cry,
"There goes Bill the Bullocky,
He's bound for Gundagai.
A better poor old — —

Never cracked an honest crust;
A tougher, poor old − −
Never drug a whip through dust."

His team got bogged at the Five-Mile Creek,
Bill lashed and swore and cried:
"If Nobby don't get me out of this, I'll tattoo his − − hide."
But Nobby strained and broke the yoke,
And poked out the leader's eye,
Then the dog sat on the tucker box,
Five miles from Gundagai.

"What is tucker?" I asked.

"Food," he replied.

I was mightily impressed by John's ability to recite poetry. It wasn't what I expected from such a straight-up-and-down young man.

We spread out a rug, and I investigated the contents of the picnic hamper. As would have been expected, it was sumptuous. There were hard-boiled eggs, which we seasoned with salt in little paper twists.

"Which relative is it that you're visiting?" asked John. "You don't have to explain if you don't want to."

He asked gravely, not in any sense displaying vicarious enjoyment of my convoluted personal life.

"If I tell you, can I ask that you keep it quiet," I replied. I was relieved that I would have a chance to talk about it. Perhaps that would still the gnawing anxiety that was growing inside me.

"Of course," he replied.

Out spilt the whole story, and I could talk about how I felt. He was a good listener, and I began to see that beyond his front of being a goody-goody, he was a quiet, thoughtful and compassionate young man. Once I released the flood of my emotions, I found myself telling him how Mummy had suggested that I hadn't had a boyfriend because I'd never had a father. This rankled more than any other part of the situation for some reason.

"Since you've trusted me with such personal information, I'll tell you something about my own situation," he said. "I'm hopelessly in love, unrequited passion for a girl at university. We're casual friends, but I can't move the situation beyond that. If it were Robbie, he'd be taking her out to the pictures and dinner, but I just don't seem to have that easy knack with women."

"Robbie seems to have a careless spirit when it comes to the fairer sex," I ventured. "If it were me, I would appreciate someone quiet and thoughtful with deep feelings. Perhaps you should just continue as you are with her. What is she like?"

"She's just perfect," he sighed. "She wears very conventional clothing, skirts or long trousers, blouses and cardigans, there's nothing bohemian about her. She studies history and spends a lot of time reading books that are not even set texts in her course. She told me that she wants to be a professor one day."

I noticed that he didn't describe her physical attributes.

"But what do you want to do when you finish university?" I asked.

I rattled on as we passed through the towns of Adelong, and then we came to Batlow, famous for its apples. Tumbarumba and we were in the mountains.

"What a splendid name!" I exclaimed, looking around with interest.

Then came Tooma, and Towong.

"Now, somewhere around here, the Mitchells live. You know Elyne Mitchell, who wrote *The Silver Brumby*," commented John.

I was in the heartland of the brumbies and the author who had told the whole world about these marvellous horses that ran wild in the Snowy Mountains.

"I do hope I get to see some brumbies," I said, not knowing to what extent this wish would come true. If wishes were horses, then beggars would ride.

We passed some large green playing fields on the outskirts of Corryong.

"That's for polocrosse. They started the Upper Murray Polocrosse Association here about ten years ago. Have you ever played?" asked John.

"No, neither that nor polo," I replied.

"It's great fun. We did some at Pony Club when we were kids. Robbie's horse, Pepperpot, was a demon. It's more accessible to the ordinary person as you only need one pony, unlike polo, where you must have a stable full for each player. You know there used to be a grand Polo Week at Yass, culminating in a Polo Ball. There would be 400 guests, the hoi poloi of the rural and equestrian society. Now that was pageantry!"

We drove through the centre of the little town.

"I'm tired, so I'm going to book in at that hotel," said John. "So, if you don't want to stay at your father's just come back up to town and I won't leave until mid-morning."

"Oh!" I said, thinking that he was doing this for me, not really because he was tired. But it did make me feel a bit safer.

By now, it was mid-afternoon. Corryong was more picturesque than some other towns we had passed through on our way here. It was the home of *The Man from Snowy River*.

At the end of town, we turned left down a dirt road and pulled up in front of a small wooden house. A man was standing on the verandah, obviously waiting for us. I thanked John for driving me and asked him not to wait. He looked like he wanted to argue, to stay and see if I was alright, but thought better of it. Clutching my overnight bag, I walked towards the house. The man who was my father stood at the top of the steps and stared into my eyes. His face was stretched into an enormous smile. There was an exuberance in that smile, more honest and intense than I had expected. It pierced through my heart. I was staring into my own reflection, into eyes that were my eyes, the same colour and shape but framed in a web of wrinkles.

"I've read your books," he said by way of introducing himself.

"My books?" I echoed.

"Your pony books about you, your mother," he stumbled momentarily over the word, "and Black Boy and Rapide. I had a friend who worked in the prison library, and I got him to order them."

I blanched at this, unable to hide my reaction. I had wondered whether or not prison should be mentioned, whether it would be more polite not to talk about it. But this unknown man, who was my father, was obviously a plain-speaker who called a spade a spade.

"I never imagined my books in a prison library," I replied.

"Thankfully, you could never imagine many aspects of prison life," he said ruefully with a friendly grin, which took the sting out of the remark.

"I've got some photos of Black Boy, Rapide, Balius and Skydiver if you're interested," I said, sounding like a doting parent who imagines their unique and marvellous offspring will be of interest to everyone in the world.

"That's great," he said.

As I showed him the photos, I realised Mummy was holding Black Boy in one of them. I was suddenly confused. Somehow, I imagined he would be devastated to see her. He did look rather intently at that photo but didn't comment.

"Let's go inside, and I'll make you a cuppa," he said. "We drink a lot of tea in the bush. It quenches the thirst in this hot weather. Then we'll fry two meaty steaks on the barbecue and fresh salad with a dressing I made myself."

"Did you know that the little horses dig for water on Sable Island, off the coast of Canada, Nova Scotia? I thought they might do that in the deserts of Australia," I suggested. This was a little random, but it was one of the topics of conversation that I had rehearsed in case there were awkward silences. The mention of being thirsty in hot weather had triggered it.

"I didn't know that," he replied quite seriously. Here in the mountains, we have snow in the winter, it's hot in the summer but not a desert."

"No, of course not."

We sat down on the front verandah to drink our tea. The dirt road was empty, no cars drove past. There was an awkward silence. I had used up my prepared speech on the Canadian horses.

"Now, tell me about your life in Chatton. I know a lot from your books, but I want to hear it from you. All the details that you didn't write about."

I burbled on, almost gabbling, elaborating on Susan Pyke who had not been my friend at school. My first struggles with Black Boy when I couldn't ride. A torrent of details flowed out of me. He listened intently and made suitable noises and comments whenever I stopped talking to catch my breath. I talked on and on. Finally, it was time for dinner.

He went out to the back garden, or backyard as they call it in Australia, and I saw that in the centre of the bare yard, he had a small metal tub set up with a glowing fire and a rack on top.

"It's best to let the flames die down and cook over the hot embers. How do you like your steak? Your mother liked hers medium," he said.

"I prefer mine a little more rare," I replied.

"There is a bowl of salad in the fridge. The salad dressing, crockery and cutlery are all ready there."

I went back inside and had the chance to look around curiously. There were only two rooms in the house. Through the open door to the bedroom, I could see a single bunk bed and a wooden orange crate set up as a bedside table with a lamp. The main room had a cast iron pot-bellied stove with a kettle hissing. It was the only type of stove for cooking. I assume that he used one pot to cook all the ingredients, or the barbecue to fry. Everything was very plain, without ornament or any type of flourishes. But clean, well-scrubbed, and manly. Nothing to be ashamed of. He carried the steaks on an enamel plate, and we sat at the table and ate. The meat was tasty, the salad fresh and crispy and white crusty bread with a pat of golden butter. He produced two brown bottles of beer and large glasses.

"Do you drink beer?" he asked. "I must admit I've developed quite a taste for it since I've been here. My social life consists only of going down to the local pub. Real men drink beer in Australia."

"I would rather just have some water," I replied. "I'm not much of a drinker. I can manage a glass of wine, but I'm perfectly happy without it."

"I should have thought of that," he apologised.

"Don't be silly. I really don't drink much," I insisted.

He knifed a thick layer of golden butter onto the bread. I watched with interest.

"Treat myself to luxuries like lots of butter. They gave us lard in the clink," he explained. "Never mind me. Did you know that my parents died three years ago. My mother used to come and visit once a month. She put aside her shame and made the journey. My father didn't visit, but he wrote to me every week. Your mother and I agreed it should be a clean break, and we would have no contact. I wanted to give her a chance to get on with her life. I thought she might marry again, but it took years."

"Yes, we moved to Oxfordshire. Looking back now, I can understand that we needed a new place where they didn't know anything about the court case. Unfortunately, there was very little money, so Mummy sold our house, and with what money she had, she bought Pool Cottage at Chatton—which is quite a decent place, really—and then she only had the little that was left and what she got from writing her children's books."

I stopped aghast. I hoped he didn't think I was blaming him for our humble and frugal life in those early years. Suddenly, I found that the story of my life was like a jigsaw puzzle. The pieces had been thrown into the air and now had to be reorganised in such a way as to create a new picture. I had only written about my father once in my first book, *Jill's Gymkhana,* and I had never mentioned him again. We were living in Wales in a big, rambling house at the foot of the hills. After his supposed death we had sold up and moved to Chatton, to our tiny cottage. I have now found out that all our money had gone into legal fees, and that is why we have begun our new life budgeting for every sixpence, as Mummy would say.

Since Mummy had shocked me to the core with the truth that my father was alive, I had tried to summon up my early childhood memories, but they were elusive. I felt as if something was there, teetering on the edge of my consciousness, but I couldn't quite grasp it. I knew that my father had been tall and lean with blonde hair. This man in front of me was aged. Although he couldn't quite be fifty, he looked much older. I guess prison life was hard, and the suffering he had gone through had left its mark.

In my books I had written about how my father had a special relationship with horses, although, by all accounts, he didn't ride them.

I sat on the sofa, and he sat in the armchair in the small living room after we had eaten dinner, and there was an awkward silence. I was just thinking that

I should get up and do the dishes when he said, "Do you want me to tell you how I ended up in prison?"

I hesitated. I didn't want to appear to be pruriently curious, but I was anxious to know, to gauge for myself exactly what had happened.

"Yes, I would. If you don't mind talking about it," I replied.

There was a moment of silence. Then he began.

"In my last year of freedom, ten years after the end of the war, it was the beginning of the era of spies, the Cold War, and the threat of the Russians. Guy Burgess and Donald Maclean had just defected and escaped to Moscow. Somehow, I got embroiled in it, totally unwittingly."

"Gosh! Mummy didn't tell me about that," I exclaimed.

"I don't think I really told her about it. It was afterwards, thinking about it, lots of time to think," he said ruefully, his blue eyes twinkling.

"Could you tell me the whole story right from the beginning," I asked. "I'm desperately curious."

"Yes, you're right. I should tell someone the story as much as I can remember and what I have been able to deduce over the years, thinking back. Are you sure you want to be subjected to it? It might be better for you to know nothing at all. Of course, I was sworn to secrecy, but I can't say that I feel loyal to my country."

I could see the black night outside the uncurtained window. I was sitting on the squashy sofa. He was comfortable in the one armchair.

"Of course, I want to know," I replied, panting with insatiable curiosity.

"I'll make us a mug of tea, and then I'll start at the beginning," he said. I noticed he put a hefty slug of something out of a small brown bottle in his tea. I suppose he needed some Dutch courage. From how he slurred his words, I thought he might be well and truly pickled.

We sat up through the night, and he told me the tale. It was probably accurate to say 'a story'. I'm not sure what was true and what was surmised, but perhaps it was an interesting invention to sweeten his memories. To put himself in a better light. To this day, I don't really know what is true.

He rambled on into the night, and I was so tired that my eyes drooped. Finally, I said I had to go to bed when he began to wend his way back to the story's beginning, like a broken record.

"You sleep in the bed. I'll bunk down on the sofa," he said.

"No," I insisted. "I'm perfectly happy on the sofa. I don't want to take your bed."

I lay on the couch. I felt like spiders were dancing on my skin, laying eggs in my brain. Outside, there were strange rustlings and cries of unfamiliar animals. I was finding it hard to understand the story I had been told. When my mother explained about my father and the death of his business partner, she did not mention anything about espionage. I was relieved that he was not a ruthless murderer. Still, I was angry that our family life had been destroyed by the evil-doing of a careless and wanton American who had used my father simply as a courier.

I saw a full summer moon lighting the monochromatic darkness through the window. I fell asleep and woke up early in the morning. I could hear him gently snoring in the bedroom. I went out to the outhouse and then sat quietly on the verandah. I didn't want to wake him. I had a lot of things to think about. It reminded me of the story of *The Railway Children* where the father had been falsely imprisoned as a spy.

I wrote down notes, such as they were, and here I will present as coherent an account as possible. This happened nine years before Kim Philby, the 'third man' in a ring of high-class British spies, famously defected to Moscow. It seemed that my father had been embroiled in a sinister plot and was the fall guy. Well, that is me gilding the lily a little or putting the best gloss on the story.

I will begin again. My father set up an advertising consultancy, which is rather a grand title for his business. He sold advertising space in various provincial newspapers and journals. He travelled around England and Wales, going to small businesses and selling them advertising space. He would help them write advertisements, and due to his artistic ability, he would sketch amusing cartoon figures. In other words, he used lithography, copywriting, and graphic design skills. The advertisements would be placed in a host of different magazines and newspapers, and for every sale, he earned a sizeable commission. He worked on his own, and he brought home the bacon for Mummy and me. We lived in a lovely house in the hills of Wales. Daddy said they were as happy as two doves coo-ing in their own little dovecote.

Then, he met a man in a pub, as people do, and he was dazzled by a vision of international glory. This man was an American called Jerry Cableton, and he was as glossy and persuasive as the most spivvy of advertisements. Everything about him smacked of the post-war promise of the Good Life. He talked about Freedom and Democracy as if it were a religion and was the most ardent of converts and proselytisers. He persuaded my father into a joint venture, and they would sell advertising not just in Britain but also in a series of newspapers that sold to ex-pats in all sorts of places that had been part of the great and glorious British Empire.

During my father's first trip to Lebanon, he had been mesmerised by this exotic country. In those days, Beirut was a hotbed of politics, and the Middle East was seething with Israeli-Arab issues, with Britain and America stirring the pot, seeing to their own interests in the rampant Cold War. My father was an innocent and had golden dreams of building an empire that rivalled J Walter Thompson, one of the world's largest and most creative advertising agencies. He was not seeing the underbelly of this world that smacked of psychological warfare, propaganda and guileful skulduggery.

He tried to describe Lebanon, and his words tumbled chaotically as if I had imagined it was in that far-off land. A melting pot of religions and nationalities: Maronite Christian, Shiite and Sunni Moslems, with a spattering of Greek Orthodox. Many Palestinians had fled from Israel and were settled in camps near the border. Nasser and his compatriots in Egypt were challenging the old colonial powers. Guns were prevalent and openly carried, and this contributed a sense of threat to the chaos and confusion.

My father's new partner took him to the St Georges bar, a regular drinking place for spies, often masquerading as British and American journalists. Jerry didn't mention this at the time, but. spies were thick on the ground, and the guard was changing as the old-world British spies were being overtaken by the new breed of American agents loaded with cash and zest to promulgate the cause of the United States in its pursuit of hegemony. The Americans were busy overthrowing established governments in Iran and meddling in Syrian politics, with the lure of enormous profits from oil spurring them on.

My father was easily led by his American partner, and he chatted with various Brits looking to establish relationships with newspapers where he might place advertisements. There was a range of 'consultants' who seemed to be promising business, but he couldn't really understand how they worked. It was a world away from dealing with local businesses in the provinces of England.

There were also many Saudi princes and glamorous wealthy Americans such as Sidney Poitier and other Hollywood greats who made appearances in the vibrant night spots such as Les Caves du Roy and the Kit Kat Club, where one dined and danced and pursued other hedonistic types of entertainment.

My father was spinning in deep waters and had no idea how to even do business in this environment, but Jerry flattered him and told him he was doing fine and would soon pick it up. After several weeks, my father told him he was returning to England he needed to attend to his ordinary business interests. He arranged to meet Jerry in London in a month or so. He gave my father a sheaf of business papers to take back with him and told him they would go through them upon his return.

My father scurried back to my mother and me in Wales. He tried to tell her what was happening, but he really didn't have a clue and couldn't figure out how he would make money in such an environment that was so far from the safe and cosy world he knew in England. My mother was dubious about his new business partner and suggested he go to London and tell him the deal was off.

He left, and the next time she was to see him was in prison. He had gone to a hotel in London and, sitting in the foyer, had begun to peruse the business papers he had brought back. He began to smell a rat. Mixed in with brochures and notes about companies that exported various Eastern goods were documents that appeared to be related to defence projects.

Jerry finally arrived, looking positively smooth to the point of oily. My father insisted that they go up to his room. He intended to confront him about the nature of the papers he had brought back into the country.

Jerry was evasive and then confrontational when my father refused to hand them over. It came down to pushing and shoving, and Jerry fell and hit his head on the corner of a solid table. He was unconscious on the floor, and my father called for help, but it was too late. His skull was cracked. The police had taken the papers, and they were never mentioned again. My father was originally charged with murder, but eventually, it was changed to manslaughter. The case had been handed over to some mysterious men in suits who spoke with upper-class accents. Eventually, it was agreed that if my father pleaded guilty, he would be eligible for early release.

Later, they visited him in prison and suggested that if he went to live in Australia, he might be out in ten or twelve years. He agreed. He told my mother he wanted a divorce and that she must go away and make a new life for herself and forget him. She had fought against this, but he was adamant, and she was hurt and weakened with the stress of everything. Finally, she agreed. I was told that he had died, and we had moved to Oxford to begin a new life without the stain of my father's sordid crime dogging our heels.

He had told me this in a rambling fashion, repeating and sometimes contradicting himself, drinking freely from his small brown bottle. For once, I didn't have much to say. I was boggling with astonishment. The veiled mention of spies and treachery had thrown me into unknown waters. Yes, I had read many Enid Blyton stories when I was younger before I graduated to pony books, and there had often been sinister foreign spies that adventurous children had caught, but I had always dismissed these stories as a type of literary invention. I had never encountered even a whisper of espionage in my ordinary life. I had once ventured into the fringes of a criminal world when I was embroiled in dog smuggling down in Cornwall, but I had walked away from that activity and never looked back.

He described prison as a world structured by ritual, almost a meditation. But not really. Underlying the scaffold of repetitive activities, there is an undercurrent of threat. At any moment, violence can erupt. Each prisoner has their agony, which manifests as anger against someone or turned inward in depression. He described his head as full of tirades of accusation. He was guilty of utter stupidity. His partner took him in. He said that for some time, he felt as if he had gone insane.

I had decided to call him David rather than Daddy. Although there had been a moment of innate recognition when I had first arrived, I now had a strong sense that he was a stranger. He was a genial and likeable man but essentially a stranger.

He woke and stumbled out of bed, and I saw he was the worse for wear. He did drink a lot. I wondered if this was simply the stress of meeting me or habitual. I decided we would leave the subject of spies and treachery and engage in a lighter conversation. Last night's spate of self-disclosure had been overwhelming. I took refuge in the endlessly fascinating topic of horses. He jumped into this subject gratefully.

Haltingly, he confessed over our mugs of tea, doorstep-sized toast, butter, and jam that he still felt close to horses. He found that he could almost hear their thoughts. I asked how this occurred. I was interested in the nuts and bolts of such communication. He looked increasingly evasive and told me that he would study the form like every responsible punter when he went to a race meeting. Still, when he wandered around the stables and looked over the contenders, they seemed to be telling him how they felt and what they thought might be their chances. He had even bet small sums on such promptings; extraordinarily, he had won quite a few times.

I stared at him in shock. It could be that he had become a hopeless gambler and a drinker. This would ensure his headlong tumble down the great heap of humanity, from ex-con to one of those seedy men who hang around racetracks and always think that their next bet will be the one that sets them straight.

I think he divined my thoughts.

"I know what you're thinking," he began.

"You can read my mind like horses," I threw back at him.

"Well, it is obvious that betting on horses can be a tricky activity, but it really does seem to work. I don't know how I really don't," he admitted ruefully. "We could go to a race meeting at Towong Racecourse, very close to here."

"Yes, we drove through it when we came yesterday."

"We can see whether the horses tell me who is going to win. Perhaps I just

had a strange run of luck, and it won't work again. Then you can chide me, and I can give up."

"Do they talk to you like Mr Ed?" I asked.

"I don't know who Mr Ed is," he replied with a puzzled expression.

"It's an American television programme. He's a horse that talks to its owner, Wilbur."

"I'm not much of a one for television," he replied.

But let me just tell you, with my winnings, I bought a broken-down old horse, and I've been teaching myself to ride. Perhaps you can give me some pointers. I believe that teaching riding is one of your gifts."

"Don't worry, I can give you some advice on riding," I said. Teaching horse riding was what I had been doing for many years, and it would be my pleasure to help my long-lost father gain the rudiments of good horsemanship. It might divert him from the racetrack and prevent him from losing all his money on betting.

"I'll take you down to see Old Joe, my horse," he said. "Leave the dishes. We can fix them when we come back. I know he's not much to look at, but I believe he is a noble old nag."

I attributed the derogative term 'nag' to the Australian idiom and followed him eagerly down the verandah steps. He went into a small shed in the yard and came out carrying what I now knew was an Australian stock saddle and a bridle with a rusty ring snaffle, but the leather had been carefully cleaned and looked supple and quite presentable. I must admit that I was taking a critical stance.

He led me through a side gate and across a small dusty paddock. There was no sign of a horse. I could hear the mournful sounds of beef cattle in the distance. There was a patch of scrub at the end of the paddock and the sharp, pungent smell of eucalyptus.

"Joe, Joe," my father called in his deep voice that seemed to blend with the noise of the cattle lowing.

A tall brown horse shambled out from the brush and whickered softly.

"This is him."

"He looks like a gentle old soul," I said. Although the horse was ribby with a pronounced backbone, his coat was shiny, and he looked happy to see us. A sure sign that he had been treated with kindness.

"He needs more feeding up. Perhaps you can advise me on that," said my father.

"Of course," I said. "He is a thoroughbred?"

"Yes, an ex-racehorse. He was quite a star in his youth, I believe."

My father ran his hand across the old horse's back, smoothing the hair, then under his belly where the girth would be fitted. He slipped the bridle over his head and then a shabby woollen saddle blanket, and the stock saddle was gently placed in the correct position and cinched carefully, ensuring the loose skin behind the elbows was not pinched.

"You seem to know what you're doing," I commented.

"There was a book in the library, and I spent hours memorising every word," he replied. "Would you like to ride him?"

"No, no, you must show me your stuff."

He put his foot in the stirrup and swung into the saddle. There was nothing to criticise in his style. The stock saddle threw him into a position where the lower leg was further forward than what was considered optimal with my riding style. It threw him further back in the seat of the saddle.

I winced when he clicked on Joe and gently shook the reins. I imagined that he had seen that watching American western movies. The big horse shambled off. His hind legs trailed behind him, the reins hanging in loops, but he was very relaxed. They circled the small paddock. Then my father took up the reins and clicked again, and they fell into a jog that resembled a very slow trot. My father sat easily in the saddle and did not attempt to rise.

Then he turned back towards me and pulled up.

"We haven't tried a canter yet," he told me. "We're just two old-timers enjoying each other's company. I would love to see you ride him. See how he goes with an expert."

"I'm up for it. That stock saddle seems to throw one to the back of the saddle, and the lower leg goes too far forward," I commented.

I adjusted the length of the stirrup leathers and mounted. Gathering the reins, I squeezed with my calves. Joe moved forward. He seemed to understand this aid.

"You don't shake the reins," commented my father.

"Now you mention it, you use the reins for various reasons but shaking them isn't a good idea to make the horse move forward. It's best to use legs to urge the horse forward. You squeeze with the calves. This is one of the reasons why having your leg too far forward is awkward: you have to move your leg back to squeeze. But never, never kick," I added.

Joe walked forward, and I took up contact with his mouth. I turned him to the left, using my right leg and the rein aid, and then turned him to the right. Surprisingly, he seemed well-schooled. I pushed him on to a trot. He shambled off, and I insisted he put more energy into his movement. I rose up and down, and we managed two entirely creditable circles.

"You're posting to the trot," called my father. "I remember reading that in the book, but I couldn't get the hang of it."

I had explained posting to the trot a million times to beginner riders in England. I never thought I would be instructing my father one day.

"The trot is a two-time movement. Diagonal fore and hind legs move together. You rise on the first beat and then sit on the next beat. You can rise on either diagonal. When you circle to the right, you look down to the outside front shoulder and rise as it moves forward. To change diagonals, you sit for one bump."

"You explain it so well," said my father, and I saw the ghost of paternal approval that seemed familiar, something that I had experienced as a child. "But how to canter. The signals to canter always seemed so confusing."

I explained the aids to him. Then, I demonstrated. I made firm contact with old Joe, and we were off. He had a surprisingly comfortable canter, and I adjusted my position to the one demanded by the stock saddle.

"Now you try," I said after we circled the paddock, and I returned to him.

What followed had a surreal quality. The hot Australian sun beat down on us. Joe's hoofs kicked up a fine dust. I gave my father a riding lesson. As you may have predicted, he was an apt pupil. He was a natural, which one would expect of a man who claimed he could communicate with horses at a high level.

Joe began to sweat as he cantered several times around the paddock, my father sitting naturally and comfortably in the saddle.

"I think it's time for Joe to rest," he said. "We can take him into the garden and wash him down with a bucket. I don't have enough water in the tank to wash him with the hose."

After tending to the old horse, we fed him chaff, crushed oats, barley, and a handful of cracked corn. He munched through his food, but I noticed he dropped quite a bit from his mouth. I suggested that his teeth might need filing to smoothe the sharp edges to make it easier for him to masticate.

We went to lunch. It was a simple meal: lettuce, tomatoes, cucumbers, tinned meat and what was unusual was tinned pineapple and beetroot. I had never eaten pineapple and beetroot in a salad, just as I hadn't eaten this combination on a hamburger, but it was very tasty.

"We can go to a race meeting tomorrow if you like?" my father suggested. Perhaps he thought I would disapprove of racing and betting.

"That would be interested!" I said.

"Tonight, we can go down to the pub and have dinner. Do you mind if I tell the chaps that you're my daughter?"

I could see that although he voiced this question casually, it meant a lot to him.

"Of course," I said. "I would be proud to be presented as your daughter."

I hadn't been to a country pub before, but it was an Australian experience that I shouldn't miss out on. Lots of men and a few weather-beaten, tough-looking women were drinking their beers. Again, we had steak, but this time, we had heated-up tinned vegetables and hot chips, and everything was lavished with tomato sauce.

Halfway through our meal, someone rushed into the pub and addressed the room in a booming voice.

"Old man Diplock's mare threw him in the scrub today, and she's gone off to the mountains and, by all accounts, will have joined the brumbies!"

This dramatic pronouncement was greeted with loud laughter.

"She's joined the wild bush horses!" shouted one.

"She's worth a thousand pound!" countered another.

"Probably more than a thousand pound. There's a reward of 500 pounds to the one who catches her," shouted out the bringer of the news.

This changed the mood.

"Where'd this happen?" asked one old-timer.

"Down by the old timber mill, and she went up the gully that leads to Upper Warriwong," replied the man.

Then followed a melee of jostling people shouting and answering each other.

"We'll gather tomorrow morning at the mill," announced one.

My father had a quiet word with one of his mates, and they agreed to lend me a horse.

"Looks like you'll be riding after the brumbies, and we're not going to the racetrack," he said with a grin. "I'm not that fast, but with my ability to communicate with horses and your experienced horsemanship, we might have a chance to catch this horse."

"Do you know the horse?" I asked. "We'll have to be able to recognise her."

"We'll be with the others anyway, and we'll have to be careful not to get lost. She's pretty distinctive, the mare, a very flashy chestnut with a white blaze, four white socks and a patch of white on her belly," replied David.

We walked back to the little house. It looked like my visit would be an occasion to be remembered. It would be much more exciting than a race meeting.

"I've got a book of Banjo's poetry here," said my father, going to a bookshelf with an extensive collection of books. "Here, have a read. Have you heard of it?"

"Yes, I have. But I can't say I've read it entirely," I said, scanning the verse.

"Read it aloud," he said. "I'm sure you've got a good speaking voice."

This seemed a strange compliment, but I read it aloud and felt a rush of blood. It was a stirring poem, and it was exciting to think we would re-enact it tomorrow.

The Man from Snowy River

There was movement at the station, for the word had passed around
That the colt from Old Regret had got away,
And had joined the wild bush horses – he was worth a thousand pound,
So all the cracks had gather to the fray.
All the tried and noted riders from the stations near and far
Had mustered at the homestead overnight,
For the bushmen love hard riding where the wild bush horses are,
And the stock-horse snuffs the battle with delight.

There was Harrison, who made his pile when Pardon won the cup.
The old man with his hair as white as snow;
But few could ride beside him when his blood was fairly up –
He would go wherever horse and man could go.
And Clancy from the Overflow came down to lend a hand,
No better horseman ever held the reins;
For never horse could throw him while the saddle-girths would stand,
He learnt to ride while droving on the plains.

And one was there, a stripling on a small and weedy beast,
He was something like a racehorse undersized,
With a touch of Timor pony – three part thoroughbred at least –
And such as are by mountain horsemen prized.
He was hard and tough and wiry – just the sort that won't say die –
There was courage in his quick impatient tread;
And he bore the badge of gameness in his bright and fiery eye,
And the proud and lofty carriage of his head.

But still so slight and weedy, one would doubt his power to stay,
And the old man said, "That horse will never do
For a long and tiring gallop – lad, you'd better stop away,
Those hills are far too rough for such as you."
So he waited sad and wistful – only Clancy stood his friend –
"I think we ought to let him come," he said;
"I warrant he'll be with us when he's wanted at the end,
For both his horse and he are mountain bred."

"He hails from Snowy River, up by Kosciusko's side,
Where the hills are twice as steep and twice as rough,
Where a horse's hoofs strike firelight from the flint stones every stride,
The man that holds his own is good enough.
And the Snowy River riders on the mountains make their home,

Where the river runs those giant hills between;
I have seen full many horsemen since I first commenced to roam,
But nowhere yet such horsemen have I seen."

So he went – they found the horses by the big mimosa clump –
They raced away towards the mountain's brow,
And the old man gave his orders, "Boys, go at them from the jump,
No use to try for fancy riding now.
And, Clancy, you must wheel them, try and wheel them to the right.
Ride boldly, lad, and never fear the spills,
For never yet was rider that could keep the mob in sight,
If once they gain the shelter of those hills."

So Clancy rode to wheel them – he was racing on the wing
Where the best and boldest riders take their place,
And he raced his stock-horse past them, and he made the ranges ring
With the stockwhip, as he met them face to face.
Then they halted for a moment, while he swung the dreaded lash,
But they saw their well-loved mountain full in view,
And they charged beneath the stockwhip with a sharp and sudden dash,
And off into the mountain scrub they flew.

Then fast the horsemen followed, where the gorges deep and black
Resounded to the thunder of their tread,
And the stockwhips woke the echoes, and they fiercely answered back
From cliffs and crags that beetled overhead.
And upward, ever upward, the wild horses held their way,
Where mountain ash and kurrajong grew wide;
And the old man muttered fiercely, "We may bid the mob good day,
No man can hold them down the other side."

When they reached the mountain's summit, even Clancy took a pull,
It well might make the boldest hold their breath,
The wild hop scrub grew thickly, and the hidden ground was full
Of wombat holes, and any slip was death.
But the man from Snowy River let the pony have his head,
And he swung his stockwhip round and gave a cheer,
And he raced him down the mountain like a torrent down its bed,
While the others stood and watched in very fear.

He sent flint stones flying, but the pony kept his feet,
He cleared the fallen timber in his stride,
And the Man from Snowy River never shifted in his seat –

It was grand to see that mountain horseman ride.
Through the stringy barks and saplings, on the rough and broken ground,
Down the hillside at a racing pace he went;
And he never drew the bridle till he landed safe and sound,
At the bottom of that terrible descent.

He was right among the horses as they climbed the further hill,
And the watchers on the mountain standing mute,
Saw him ply the stock whip fiercely, he was right among them still,
As he raced across the clearing in pursuit.
Then they lost him for a moment, where two mountain gullies met
In the ranges, but a final glimpse reveals
On a dim and distant hillside the wild horses racing yet,
With the man from Snowy River at their heels.

And he ran them single-handed till their sides were white with foam.
He followed like a bloodhound on his track,
Till they halted cowed and beaten, then he turned their heads for home,
And alone and unassisted brought them back.
But his hardy mountain pony he could scarcely raise a trot,
He was blood from hip to shoulder from the spur;
But his pluck was still undaunted, and his courage fiery hot,
For never yet was mountain horse a cur.

And down by Kosciusko, where the pine-clad ridges raise
Their torn and rugged battlements on high,
Where the air is clear as crystal, and the white stars fairly blaze
At midnight in the cold and frosty sky,
And where around the Overflow the reedbeds sweep and sway
To the breezes, and the rolling plains are wide,
The man from Snowy River is a household word to-day,
And the stockmen tell the story of his ride.

By 'The Banjo', Andrew Barton Paterson

"You know the poem was supposed to be based on a local character, Jack Riley. He lived up in the mountains in a small hut. He knew the mountains like no one else," said David. "The legend of Jack Riley, the Man from Snowy River, is extremely important to Corryong. Last century, he lived up in the mountains at Tom Groggin, near Leatherbarrel Mountain and Dead Horse Gap. But there are other contenders for the role."

"What wonderful names!" I exclaimed. "Do you think I'll be mounted on a weedy thoroughbred?" I asked, my blood stirred at the words.

"Probably," he said. "You know there is a theory that it wasn't Jack Riley who was the Man from Snowy River but a man called Charlie McKeahnie. Another poet who signed his work as 'Surcingle' wrote a different poem with a very similar story, and it actually alludes to the hero by name, 'Charlie Mac'. I'll recite this other ballad, much less known, but isn't it interesting that there are so many points of similarity?"

On The Range

On Nungar the mists of the morning hung low,
The beetle-browed hills brooded silent and black,
Not yet warmed to life by the sun's loving glow,
As through the tall tussocks rode Charlie Mac.
What cared he for mists at the dawning of day,
What cared he that over the valley stern "Jack,"
The Monarch of frost, held his pitiless sway?--
A bold mountaineer born and bred was young Mac,
A galloping son of a galloping sire –
Stiffest fence, roughest ground, never took him aback;
With his father's cool judgement; his dash, and his fire,
The pick of Manaro rode young Charlie Mac.
And the pick of the stable the mare he bestrode –
Arab-grey, built to stay, lithe of limb, deep of chest,
She seemed to be happy to bear such a load
As she tossed the soft forelock that curled on her crest.
They crossed Nungar Creek where its span is but short
At its head, where together sprang two mountain rills,
When a mob of wild horses sprang up with a snort –
"By thunder!" quoth Mac, "there's the Lord of the Hills,"
Decoyed from her paddock, a Murray-bred mare,
Had fled to the hills with a warrigal band,
A pretty bay foal had been born to her there,
Whose veins held the very best blood in the land –
"The Lord of the Hills" as the bold mountain men
Whose courage and skill he was wont to defy
They named him, they yarded him once, but since then
He held to the saying, "Once bitten, but twice shy."

The scrubber, thus suddenly roused from his lair,
Struck straight for the timber with fear in his heart,
As Charlie rose up in his stirrups, the mare
Sprang forward, no need to tell Empress to start.

She laid to the chase just as soon as she felt
Her rider's skill'd touch, light, yet firm, on the rein;
Stride for stride, lengthened wide, for the green timber belt,
The fastest half-mile ever done on the plain,
They reached the low sallee before he could wheel
The warrigal mob; up they dashed with a stir
Of low branches and undergrowth – Charlie could feel
His mare catch her breath on the side of the spur
That steeply slopes up till it meets the bald cone.
'Twas here on the range that the trouble began,
For a slip on the sidling, a loose rolling stone,
And the chase would be done; but the bay in the van
And the little grey mare were a sure-footed pair
He looked once around as she crept to his heel,
And the swish that he gave his long tail in the air
Seemed to say, "Here's a foeman well worthy my steel."

They raced to within half of a mile of the bluff
That drops to the river, the squadron strung out –
"I wonder" quoth Mac, "has the bay had enough,"
But he was not left very much longer in doubt,
For the Lord of the Hills struck a spur for the flat
And followed it, leaving his mob, mares and all,
While Empress, (brave heart, she could climb like a cat)
Down the stony descent raced with never a fall.
Once down on the level 'twas galloping ground,
For a while Charlie thought he might yard the big bay
At his uncle's out-station, but no! He wheeled round
And down the sharp dip to the Gulf made his way,

Betwixt those twin portals, that, towering high
And backwardly sloping in watchfulness, lift
Their smooth grassy summits to the far sky,
The course of the clear Murrumbidgee runs swift;
No time then to seek where the crossing might be,
It was in at the one side and out where you could
But fear never dwelt in the hearts of those three
Who emerged from the shade of the low muzzle-wood.
Once more did the Lord of the Hills strike a line
Up the side of the range, and once more he looked back,
So close were they now he could see the sun shine
In the bold grey eyes flashing of young Charlie Mac.
He saw little Empress, stretched out like a hound

On the trail of its quarry, the pick of the pack.
With ne'er tiring stride, and his heart gave a bound,
As he saw the lithe stockwhip of young Charlie Mac
Showing snaky and black on the neck of the mare,
In three hanging coils, with a turn round the wrist;
And he heartily wished himself back in his lair
'Mid the tall tussocks beaded with chill morning mist.

Then he fancied the straight mountain-ashes, the gums,
And the wattles, all mocked him and whispered, "You lack
The speed to avert cruel capture, that comes
To the warrigal fancied by young Charlie Mac.
For he'll yard you, and rope you, and then you'll be stuck
In the crush, while his saddle is girthed to your back,
Then out in the open, and there you may buck
Till you break your bold heart, but you'll never throw Mac!"
The Lord of the Hills at the thought felt the sweat
Break over the smooth summer gloss of his hide;
He spurted his utmost to leave her, but yet
The Empress crept up to him, stride upon stride,
No need to say Charlie was riding her now,
Yet still for all that he had something in hand,
With here a sharp stoop to avoid a low bough,
Or quick rise and fall, as a tree-trunk they spanned.
In his terror the brumby struck down the rough falls
T'wards Yiack, with fierce disregard for his neck —
'Tis useless, he finds, for the mare overhauls
Him slowly, no timber could keep her in check.

There's a narrow-beat pathway, that winds to and fro
Down the deeps of the gully, half-hid from the day,
There's a turn in the track where the hop-bushes grow
And hide the grey granite that crosses the way;
While sharp swerves the path round the boulder's broad base,
And now the last scene in the drama is played;
As the Lord of the Hills, with the mare in full chase.

Swept t'wards it, but, ere his long stride could be stayed,
With a gathered momentum that gave not a chance
Of escape, and a shuddering, sickening shock,
He struck on the granite that barred his advance
And sobbed out his life at the foot of the rock;
While Charlie pulled off with a twitch of the rein,

And an answering spring from his surefooted mount,
One might say, unscathed, though a crimsoning stain
Marked the graze of the granite, but that would ne'er count
With Charlie, who speedily sprang to the earth
To ease the mare's burden, his deft-fingered hand
Unslackened her surcingle, loosened tight girth,
And cleansed with a tussock the spurs' ruddy brand.

There he lay by the rock – drooping head, glazing eye,
Strong limbs stilled for ever; no more would he fear
The tread of a horseman; no more would he fly
Through the hills with his harem in rapid career.
The pick of the "Mountain Mob," bays, greys, or roans,
He proved by his death that the pace 'tis that kills,
And a sun-shrunken hide o'er a few whitened bones
Marks the last resting place of the Lord of the Hills.

By 'Surcingle,' Barcroft Boake

After his recitation, I clapped. Australian poetry was emotionally stirring, especially on the night before we were to go hunting the brumbies.

"You've got a copy of *The Silver Brumby*," I said, looking through his volumes on the bookshelf.

"Yes. You know the Mitchells have a property at Towong," he replied. "Everyone knows them."

"Mummy gave me a copy of this book, and I've been reading it," I said. "I've got it here in my bag."

I scanned his other titles.

"But what is this, *The Magic Pudding*, that sounds original?"

"Technically, it's a children's book, but it is entertaining and extremely Australian. The author, Norman Lindsay, was probably the most famous Australian artist. He lived in the Blue Mountains, west of Sydney."

I leafed through the book, and it did look fascinating.

"Come on early to bed, and I'll set the alarm. In the morning, we'll go down to the pub and get a lift to the mill. They're bringing a truck for the horses. I might just go and give Old Joe an extra feed tonight. He's going to need his strength for tomorrow," said David.

That had been the sensible plan, but somehow, we weren't quite ready to sleep. I went down the paddock to help feed Old Joe, and then we sat up and continued talking. There suddenly seemed so much to talk about. David described life and the goings-on in his little town, Corryong. He seemed to have embraced life in this rural community. In some respects, it was similar to Chatton in that any small community has its customs, rituals and social network, but in other ways, it is different. There was an annual festival for the Man from Snowy River. The town was firmly rooted in its heritage, which was made famous by the poem by Banjo Patterson. There was even an event where they selected a Queen of The Man from Snowy River Festival. The contestants wore long evening dresses and gloves to their elbows, and the Queen was awarded a very fancy sash. I did think it was a bit weird that women might be judged as if they were show ponies. I can imagine what Dinah Dean would have to say about that!

Then I remembered when Ann had won the prize for the Best Dressed Child event.

"We did have something a bit like that in Chatton," I said. "A woman offered a special prize for the best-dressed child rider at the Rectory garden party, which was raising funds for mending the church steeple. I stood aloof and refused to enter into such nonsense, and fortunately, having a sensible mother who understood how I felt, there was no pressure for me to enter, but some of the other mothers were simply crackers about it. Secrets abounded, and some girls were hauled off to exclusive London tailors. Poor old Ann was forced by her mother to enter, but I have to say her outfit was impeccable - new cord breeches and boots, a covert coat, a new white shirt, string gloves and a bowler. There were some utterly ridiculous get-ups. One girl had a Charles the Second huntswoman outfit, all flowing green velvet with ostrich feathers in her hat, which unfortunately became detached, fell off and got trampled the second time around the ring. Another girl wore scarlet jodhpurs and a sort of white Hussar tunic. But it was Susan Pyke, my *bete noire,* who stole the show all in black, with silver epaulettes, a silver stripe down her breeches, patent leather boots, and crowned with a woman's hunting topper and on her hands enormous gauntlets like a Guardsman's. She was riding her father's black horse, Punch, which was much too big for her, and I unashamedly laughed uproariously when she ended up on the horse's neck, lost her stirrups, and spoiled the whole effect."

David paid attention to my story and looked wistful. Perhaps he was sad that he had missed these village events that had made up the fabric of my childhood life in Chatton.

"Speaking of horse events, you know the original horse called Garryowen was bred up here at Khancoban Station," he countered and told me the story behind the Garryowen Perpetual Trophy that had been awarded since 1934 at the Melbourne Royal Show. It is the most prestigious equestrienne event in the Australian show horse calendar. It was awarded as a tribute to Violet Murrell, a flat-racing and jump jockey and a well-known show horsewoman.

Violet's beloved horse, Garryowen, had been awarded Champion Hack several times at the Melbourne Royal and Sydney Royal Shows. There had been a fire at her stables, and she had dashed in to rescue her beloved horses, including Garryowen and her dog. She had not survived, and her husband, who also rushed into the fire to aid her, had died several days later, suffering from extensive burns.

We stayed up for hours recounting anecdotes, and it was very enjoyable. Nothing would make up for how we had missed many years of each other's lives, but it did seem to forge some bonds between us.

Chapter Twelve – Up Into the Mountains

It was dark when we got up in the morning.

"I've made some hard-boiled eggs with a fudgy yolk, the only acceptable kind of boiled egg. And some crispy bacon," said David.

"We're going to need our strength. Have we got bread and something for sandwiches to take with us?" I asked.

"There's enough bacon here to make sandwiches as well," said David.

"Oh, delicious. I love crispy bacon."

"I've packed up some other stores. Perhaps you might want to take your toothbrush, hairbrush, spare clothes, and I'll pack a towel. You know we could be several days up in the mountains. I've got a swag for you, and I'll hunker down in blankets around the campfire. We can telegram your hosts at the property near Goulburn and let them know that you might be several days away. I can borrow a car to take you to join them at the next show where you're due to compete when we get back. Give me a chance to see you showjumping. That would be a rare treat."

"Yes, I guess so," I replied. I wasn't sure how polite it was to casually tell the Heywards I would join them later, but the chance to ride in the mountains was too much of an opportunity to miss. There was also the thought of explaining who David was, 'this is my long-lost father'. "The next show is at Tamworth, and they plan to be there for three days, then we go west, inland, to a place called Bourke."

"I can send a telegram, handing it in at the general store," replied David. "Do you want to write it out?"

"Yes, that's a good idea," I said.

We saddled up Old Joe with saddlebag on either side, and the swag buckled behind the saddle. I carried a bag that could be attached to the saddle of the horse I would be lent. Then we led Joe to the pub. The truck was backed up against a high spot, and all the horses obediently stepped onto the tray and were each hooked by their bridles to the side slats. We piled into the double cab and trundled off. We went through a tiny settlement where there was a large eerie lake. Dead trees, looking like sepulchral statues, rose from the still grey water. It looked like a pen and wash illustration of simple lines with hues of brown and grey. It had an ethereal effect.

We drove into the mountains to the Old Mill. There were lots of horses and riders milling around. The stockmen's hats were pulled down low, shadowing their eyes. I was given a scruffy-looking brown pony with a stock saddle. Despite it being summer, there was a bracing chill in the air. This was the famous High Country sprinkled with pale-barked snow gums.

There was some general discussion about where the brumbies might be. Old man Diplock had been riding the chestnut mare along the track from the Old Mill across his lease, where his cattle grazed through the summer. They said he had been out checking on his stockmen, who were keeping an eye on his herd. These men had found him with a broken leg on the track, and the chestnut mare had gone, high-tailed it up to the mountains.

"Stupid ter be ridin' tha' mare in this country. She's a thoroughbred who won races, and she was to be sent orf to stud next spring ter breed a Melbourne Cup winner, so they say," said Curly, his lip curled in a snarl. Other men grunted in agreement, but few spoke out against Mr Diplock.

But there is always an exception. A sly greasy chap said something about a 'pommie blighter'.

"Most of us are from pommie stock, but they transport'd tha best of us back in tha 1700s," replied Curly with a nasty look shot at David and Jill. "So wot are yer doin' up 'ere, girly?" he said, turning on me with his squinty eyes glaring malevolently.

I was startled. I could feel his spite like a physical cut with a sharp knife. "I'm just here to join in the hunt for the mare," I replied, suddenly very conscious of my British accent, which marked me as an outsider.

"No place fer the likes of you," said Curly, as if he would gladly send me packing.

"My daughter has as much right to help in the search as anyone," declared my father robustly. He could have added that he had been transported more recently, but that would have put the cat amongst the pigeons.

"We're off along tha track wot Diplock was riding, see if we can pick up tha mare's trail, figger out which way she might have gorn," announced an older man who acted like the leader of the group. This dispelled the gathering clouds of disruption.

Some minutes later, we set off. The weather had changed. No more bright blue skies, but dark clouds roiled to the west with a strong gusty wind. The air was charged with unnamed emotions; the caress of the wind upon my face meant something, but I couldn't decipher the message—more of a puzzling tug of wild exaltation. I could feel it in the horses. It was like going out fox hunting in Britain. But these horses seemed closer to their wild ancestors than Britain's plodding cobs and well-mannered sturdy hunters.

"It might be your only chance of seeing the brumbies," David explained. "They're wary of ridden horses and men. They consider us natural enemies."

We spread out in single file along the track. I was riding behind a tall man with an extraordinarily long beard. It reached down almost to his waist and reminded me of the Ancient Mariner. He was mounted on a stocky leopard-spotted horse. Even following a trail was hard going, and the horses had to step over fallen branches. The tussocky grass looked not only unappetising but was another hazard for all but the most sure-footed mount.

I found it hard to see the track we were actually following. A myriad of smaller tracks branched off and criss-crossed our path. In one of the clearings, there was a small mob of cattle. They were sleek and fat, well-bred Herefords. Although the grazing up here didn't look like the lush green fields of Oxfordshire, there must have been good nutrition in the mountain grasses.

We were climbing higher, following a ridge. Then we turned up through a gully. We splashed our way upwards through one of the many small streams that ran erratically down the mountains. Now and then we caught sight of the country below us but most of the time high mountain walls and thick bush enclosed us. I was thankful that I had been lent a tough little mountain horse. He was indeed a 'weedy thoroughbred' and he seemed entirely undaunted by the hard going. I gave him a long rein and leaned slightly forward as we moved uphill, trusting him to pick his way.

For three hours our horses took us through the bush. The higher we got the sparser the trees and shrubs, but the ground was littered with strips of bark and branches. These gum trees were evergreen but the messiest things I had ever seen. Bits and pieces of them were constantly littering the ground. Eventually, we came to a plateau. We were not at the top of the range but there was a panoramic view. From here we could look back at the series of hillsides that we'd climbed. In the distance to the south was a range of hills, and beyond them another range, and then another range, a succession of blues. A few of the men took binoculars out of their saddle bags and most others scanned the bush with narrowed eyes looking for any movement that could be horses.

According to *The Silver Brumby* wild animals and birds cried news like a bush telegraph. If this were true then the brumbies would have been alerted to our presence in the mountains long before we came across them, even if we managed to approach downwind. We came to the place where Mr Diplock had fallen and from there, we spread out searching for clues of which way the mare might have gone.

"Ere! Ere!" shouted Curly. "Look, there's droppin's 'ere. She went this way, off up tha' mountain. Come on!"

We set off in a bunch. There was a general air of excitement rippling through the mob of us. We were now on the trail. Curly took charge, riding first and looking for more signs of where the mare might have gone. I did wonder

how it would pan out if we found her. Presumably the man who got the rope around her neck would get the reward. I imagined that Curly was determined to be that person.

On we rode until the afternoon shadows were long. Still, there was no sign of any horses: neither the chestnut mare nor any brumbies.

"We'll camp at tha' 'ut up on tha' ridge," shouted one of the men, pointing his stock whip towards the crest of the mountain.

There was a small creek running near the hut and we dismounted and unsaddled the horses. David took Old Joe and my mount, who was called Sinbad, and suggested that I take our gear and go up to the hut and work out where we were going to sleep.

Outside the hut were two lean-tos which were stocked with firewood, sealed drums of flour, and other supplies. Inside the hut there were two good-sized rooms with a wide opening between them, no door. The walls were lined with old newspapers that somewhat plugged the gaps between the timbers. Hessian sacks formed a canopy under the ceiling. The floor was made of the same split logs that were used for the walls and a stone fireplace took up one entire side. There was even a spotty mirror and a green enamel medicine cabinet propped beside three kerosene lamps.

Two men were busying themselves arranging small logs in the fireplace with old newspaper crumpled around some kindling. They put a match to it and reassuring yellow flames licked around the logs.

"We'll need a fire ternight," one of them said, "it gets cold up 'ere in tha evening."

I looked around and wondered how everyone might find their own place to sleep. I had the swag and the blankets.

"You might want to put tha' swag down this wall, next to tha blankets. Close ter tha fire," said the younger man. He'd taken off his hat and had lustrous blond locks and startling green eyes. With a shock, I realised how handsome he was, compared to the grizzled old bushmen who made up most of the group.

"I'm Jill," I blurted out.

"Frankie, at ya service," he grinned.

I was nonplussed by this. My mind was always hovering around the idea of Frank Stabley and here was a Frankie. An absolutely gorgeous handsome young man called Frankie, in truth far more handsome than Frank Stabley. Mentally I shook myself. There was no time for romance, or in my case unspoken romantic thoughts. I was on a mammoth adventure, and we were searching for a valuable horse in these wild mountains. But somehow, this was a fitting scene for romance.

Carefully I laid out the swag, and then about 18 inches away I spread out the blankets for David. From what I could see we would be packed like sardines in this small hut.

One of the men came in with some food, the camp cook. He pulled out a slab of fresh beef and began to slice it in generous steaks. He went outside and came back with a round circle of steel that he sat over the fire as a cooking surface. Then there were spuds which he put to one side. He took a large cast iron pot and hung it from a hook above the stove.

"We'll 'av the steak first an' I'll put the spuds in when tha fire 'as died down to embers," he said. "I'll start tha magic stew with the trimmin's of beef an' any leftovers.

"What's a magic stew?" I asked innocently.

"They add rabbits tha' get trapped an' tha leftovers, bits an' pieces every day. Never reach the bottom of the pot, will feed everyone for weeks."

I gulped. It sounded like a cauldron of poison after a few days. But tonight, the meat smelled delicious sizzling away.

"Rare, please," I said in a jocular manner.

"Listen ter tha' little lady thinks she dinin' out, givin' instructions ta tha servant," said the nasty Curly coming in to hear my comment.

"I was just…" I protested and then shut up. What was the point of trying to explain. No matter what I said Curly obviously had it in for me.

I had two enamel plates and two forks and knives in the bag that David had packed. The cook plonked two giant steaks on the plates and smiled at me.

"Take no mind to tha' Curly," he said in an undertone. "'E's one of them brumby 'unters. 'ope ya like tha beef."

"Without his hat he is bald, why is he called Curly?" I asked.

"It's Australian, opposites, ya know. E's bald, so e's Curly, like a red-haired man is call'd Bluey.'

"This steak looks divine," I said and could have kicked myself for sounding so prissy.

David came in ten minutes later. "I've tethered the horses, very securely," he added.

"Here's your steak," I said.

"Bonza," he commented, using his newly-learned Australian accent.

Men were crowding into the hut, laying out swags and blankets across the floor.

"I'll star' a fire outside," said one of the men. "For those who ain't goin' ta fit in 'ere."

"I might just go out and check on our horses," I said.

"Right-o," replied David.

Outside the sun had slipped down behind the mountains, leaving only a strange purple light with thin streaks of orange. There were a few bright stars in the sky and the moon was rising, a giant silver orb that would light up the night. I had never slept in such a wild place, and I felt the majesty of the mountains rising around me.

Old Joe and Sinbad had palled up together. They were dozing lightly, nodding their heads. They had been given a pile of oats on the ground in front of them which they had hoovered up. I thought that perhaps I should lead them out to find something for them to graze but then had second thoughts, better not untie them.

"Everything OK?" said a voice behind me. A deep melodious voice, I was sure it would be Frankie. I didn't dare to hope that he had followed me out. "Look at tha' moon! It's 'uge ternight."

"Wonderful," I said, feeling a rush of nervousness, breathless with a dry mouth. "What's a brumby hunter? One of the men said that Curly was a brumby hunter."

"Ah. They chase the brumbies, catch the good 'uns, shoot sum of 'em."

"Shoot them!" I exclaimed. "What on earth for?"

"They get hired by tha lease holders. They doan like tha wild horses, they eat tha feed they wan' fer their cattle."

"So they're not just here to catch the chestnut mare. They're going after the other horses."

"Tha' be right," he said, staring contemplatively into the middle distance.

"Are you one of the brumby hunters?" I asked suspiciously.

"Nah," he said.

"I better get back in," I said suddenly embarrassed by the way I had asked the question. He let me go but I could feel him watching me as I stumbled back to the hut.

David had already rolled himself in one blanket, the other spread out beneath him. I was glad of the swag. There was a thin foam mattress and a sleeping bag inside the canvas. I felt as cosy as a bug in a rug. The rooms were full of men grumbling away, cigarettes and pipes were lit and there was an unhealthy hazy fug which we would have to breathe in all night. I thought that it would be hard to sleep but I slipped away into the world of nod within minutes. I didn't stir all night. It must have been the mountain air.

I woke very early. I could see the sun peeping over the horizon through the open door and the cook was making mugs of tea. I took one gratefully, pulled on my boots, determined to go out and let the horses graze. They couldn't go up and down through the mountains on an empty stomach. Someone had given all the horses a morning feed of oats each and when Old Joe and Sinbad had snaffled theirs up I untied their ropes and led them down towards the river. I let them drink and found some dry grass a little further along the bank. Looping their ropes securely around a large fallen branch I went back to the stream and squatted down. The water was as clear as glass, slipping over metallic-looking stones. I splashed it across my face. I had thought it might be refreshing but it was frigid, too cold for comfort but hopefully good for my complexion.

The horses cropped enthusiastically. I sat down near them and stared at the burbling creek. The air smelled fresh, exhilarating and the scent of eucalyptus was strong. This was an amazingly strange world. I wondered what it might be like to live up here. No wonder the mountain people were tough. It would not be an easy life.

Suddenly the horses threw up their heads and looked across the creek to the high ground on the next hill. Their ears were pricked, and they were standing to attention. I followed their gaze and saw the outline of a large horse standing on the crest. I screwed up my eyes to see him better. He was alone, standing four square, alert, nostrils flared. I felt sure he was a wild stallion who was watching us. He must have known that we had been here all night. He would have left his herd somewhere safe and come to check out the enemies.

I didn't know what to do. I sat there watching. After a few minutes I heard him snort, paw the ground with one fore foot and then he swung on his haunches and disappeared.

I took the horses back to camp, tied them up and went in search of David. Franky was sipping a mug of tea outside the hut.

"I've just seen a big horse watching us from over there," I said pointing to the far hill. "Would he be the stallion?"

"Could be," he replied. "Ya can show us which way' e went when we ge' goin'. Ya should go in an' ge' yer bacon an' bread, need a good feed before we set out."

"Good thinking," I said, going inside the hut.

I showed Curly and some of the others where I had seen the lone stallion, and we all rode up to the top of the hill. They scouted around and found his tracks and we set off on our second day's riding. The ground was hard and stony and there weren't many tracks, but we rode through countless gullies, along the ridges and every now and again came to high ground where we could survey the bush around us.

In the late afternoon the men who knew this country well guided us to another hut. This one was more rudimentary and there was some discussion about who should sleep indoors and who on the ground outside around a campfire. Several of the men insisted that I should be inside due to being of the fairer sex. David said that he would be fine wrapped in his blanket by the fire. I was embarrassed at being singled out like this. There were a couple of other women in our number, but they were treated as equals by the men.

After dinner I went to snuggle into my swag. I lay there for a minute then experienced a strange slithering feeling around my legs. I froze in terror. It was a snake in my swag! Then, at the speed of light, I wriggled out screaming. The men quickly came to my aid. David was there his fists clenched perhaps thinking that someone was taking advantage of me.

"Snake! Snake!" I shouted, shuddering with terror.

"Were ya bitt'n?" asked one of the old blokes. Out of the corner of my eye I saw Curly grinning maliciously.

"It's only an ol' carpet snake," proclaimed the guy who had fished out the snake with a long stick which he held aloft with a huge creature sinuously waving its body around.

There was general laughter.

"But how did it get in there?" I demanded plaintively.

"Jus' must 'ave been wantin' sum female company," sneered Curly.

Then it dawned on me. It had been him who had put it there. I was determined never to crawl into a swag again but then saw that there was no alternative. I had to sleep. It was distinctly chilly, and I needed to prove that I was not a hoity toity miss from the Old Country.

The next morning, I got up early and went down to untie our horses so that they might graze on a patch of juicy green grass that I had found. It was too much to hope that the stallion might show himself again. Anyway, there was no proof that this particular stallion would know the whereabouts of the missing chestnut mare that we were looking for.

David came walking down behind me.

"I was thinking we don't seem to be getting very far in finding that mare. Perhaps you and I can strike out on our own. That way if we do find her and manage to catch her then we'll get the credit and there will be no dispute about the reward. I thought we might go better on our own."

He didn't say anything about the snake but perhaps he was thinking that I might feel better to get away from the loathsome Curly who seemed to have it in for me from the off.

"That Curly is a brumby hunter and some of the other men must be too," I said. "They're planning on capturing other horses and they'll shoot some of them. But are you sure we're not going to get lost?"

"I see your point. Obviously, there's men who know this bush and have been riding here for years. We're both new chums at this game. But I brought a map at the general store when I sent your telegram. I've been plotting our course and I've got a compass. Here look."

He spread out a map. He had plotted the way that we had come so far.

"This is pretty clever," I replied. "How did you know to do this?"

"I read quite a few books on navigation and map reading, before, you know. You can see that we're following a circular route between these two mountains. I get the feeling that the others are planning to go on this way. What if we head down to this lower country over here," he said pointing to an area that might not be as rough as the one we had been travelling across. "If I were a wild horse I would be grazing on these flats in the summer, to fill up on good grass for the hardship of the coming winter."

"Well, it seems like it's as likely the horses are there, as much as they might be in this rough mountain country," I replied thoughtfully. Really, I didn't have a clue where the brumbies might be.

"We can spend some time scouting around for tracks. The chestnut mare is shod, or she was when she got away. I don't imagine it will take long before she loses her shoes. If we can't find her then we'll be able to make our way back round here to the Old Mill where some of Mr Diplock's men are staying."

"Sounds good to me. But do we have supplies we can take?" I asked.

"Yes, I brought some and I can fish and also I've got the rifle. We can always shoot ourselves something to eat," he said. "And also, a billy to make the tea, and a tomahawk, not to mention several boxes of matches wrapped in oilskin to keep them dry."

It still sounded very basic to me. Shooting animals, skinning them and roasting them over an open fire but that was the way of the bush, and it would certainly be a novel experience.

"I'll have a word with that old man, Sonny Jim they call him. Let him know we'll be leaving the group. Don't think anyone will have any objections. It's each man for himself at the end of the day."

"Curly will be glad to see the back of me," I muttered, thinking that the feeling would be mutual.

We gathered up our gear and set off soon after breakfast. I made sure that I ate double size portions of the fried eggs and bacon. It might be lean rations after this.

Chapter Thirteen – Striking Out on Our Own

We rode off following a course due west, following the sun as it arced over the sky above us. According to the map and David's calculation, this would lead us to lower country. If nothing else, it would be easier going. We rode eyes glued to the ground, searching for the brumbies' tracks. We could find nothing. Then, I noticed something extraordinary. The most enormous pile of horse poo. It was shaped like a giant ants' nest.

"What on earth is that?" I asked.

"That is heartening," replied David. "It's where the stallion leaves his mark, a corner of his territory. It might not be the herd joined by the chestnut mare, but it is where a herd is grazing."

Then, our luck turned bad. A storm was brewing with a threatening louring sky. Far-off thunder was growling in the distance. It began to rain. There was no introductory drizzle, but an inundation fell in icy horizontal sheets. The wind slapped at our faces with icy hands. The horses were restive as we travelled directly into the rain, and they kept trying to turn their rumps to the onslaught. We came to what had been a tinkling stream of clear mountain water, and it was now roaring and rising, with a black oily look as it rushed past. We managed to wade the horses across, and I could feel the current pulling us to send us spinning downstream, but the horses doggedly kept their feet and got us safely across.

"Let's get to higher ground away from the river, huddle beside a tree and let the horses stand the way they want. They know how to protect themselves," said David.

We found a snow gum with a broad trunk and huddled on the eastern side. I leaned against the smooth, pale grey bark. I hoped the rain would stop, but it got worse. It turned first to sleet and then to hailstones as huge as golf balls. But I kept my mouth shut. I didn't want to complain, and nothing I said would change our situation, certainly not plaintive regrets that we hadn't set out on this big adventure that was quickly becoming a nightmare. If we had been in Oxfordshire or even the Scottish Highlands, there would have been a house, cottage, or croft where we could have sought shelter. There were the odd stockmen's huts with supplies if you were lucky up here, but no welcoming lights and smoke from warm fireplaces.

The rain didn't stop but began to ease.

"I think we need to get going. Find a place where we can shelter," said David. "I saw a cave marked on the map. It's quite famous, supposedly where a bushranger who used to roam here many years ago, used to shelter."

I rose to my feet. My limbs seemed to have frozen, and I found it hard to walk. At least moving would give me back some feeling. I had been wearing a thin jacket, but it was soaking wet, and I could feel the dampness going right through to my skin. My jods were clinging to my legs, and my boots were full of water.

"We should have got you one of those long oilskin coats with a cape divided around the legs so you can ride comfortably," said David.

"I'll remember for next time," I muttered. This was the inclement and unpredictable mountain weather that I had heard the men talk about. We had abandoned any semblance of civilisation. Or so I thought. Miraculously, I saw a stone chimney ahead. There must be a hut. Hope surged, and my breath quickened.

"Look! Look! Up ahead, that shape must be a chimney. A hut!"

We rode on full of hope. The afternoon was waning, and although the summer evenings were long, the sky was grey, and darkness would fall within a few hours. It was hard to see through the misty rain, and finally, we reached what was, indeed, a stone chimney, carefully constructed, standing faithful and upright. But nothing else. The hut itself was not there. A few blackened timbers showed us that the wooden structure had been burned to the ground, and all that was left was the stone chimney. It could provide us with neither shelter nor warmth.

"Do you know where that cave is?" I asked peevishly.

"I know it will be on higher ground. We must make our way upwards. See over there, the higher slope. I think that might be where we will find it," replied David hesitatingly.

"Think!" I couldn't help snapping at him. I was freezing and feeling very afraid. To stay out all night with soaking clothes was a scary and bone-chilling thought.

"I remember them saying the caves were near an old burnt hut. Let's hope we're on the right track," replied David in measured tones, not responding to my sharp, nervous comments.

We pushed the horses on. They were weary and not very willing. I tried to buck up, be a good example to the animals, and keep my spirits up. Ridiculously, I sang, "Onward Christian soldiers, marching .." I had forgotten the words to that stirring hymn we had often sung in the local church when Mummy and I had attended services.

Then David chipped in. He had a fine baritone voice. The Welsh men were known as good singers. Anyone seeing us might have thought us batty. I didn't care. If only there were other people around. Even Curly might have been a welcome sight, but we were utterly alone in the wilderness. Finally, when I had given up hope, we saw a steep mountain slope rising just ahead of us.

"Do you see that dark patch? I think that might be the mouth of a cave," said David.

My eyes searched wearily in the gathering dusk. As we got closer, I thought that perhaps he might be right. I hoped that the cave would be big enough to take the horses in, that it might be waterproof, not with gaping holes in the roof, and as wet as the bush around us.

We followed a tiny trail through the undergrowth. Perhaps the small animals, wallabies and wombats used this path up to the cave. It was the best we could hope for. Then, there was a burst of cackling laughter.

"What on earth is that?" I asked, feeling as if the spirits of the bush were laughing at our predicament.

"It's kookaburras!" said David, smiling at me. "The Aborigines think that they have a mirthful spirit."

"Let's hope they're laughing with us and not at us," I muttered. My desire to experience new and strange things was flattened. I wanted to be somewhere warm, familiar and safe.

"You know I've seen the parent kookaburras lining up their young chicks along a branch, teaching them to laugh," said David. I grunted. I was in no mood to appreciate the vagaries of bush animals.

Finally, we reached the mouth of a cave. It was large enough to lead in the horses. It was not homely, quite damp, but at least it was sheltered from the rain and wind. We untacked the horses and used the towel I had brought to rub them down. David paid particular attention to their ears.

"I read somewhere that if they have cold ears, it makes them cold all over," he explained.

We piled the tack on one side. There was nothing to tie the horses up, and there was a chance they might wander out into the night, but on balance, it seemed best to trust that they preferred to stay in the shelter. David rigged up a rope strung across the entrance, tied to two large rocks just in case. It wasn't the most substantial barrier, but hopefully, it would be enough to keep them inside. Then, I found a small entrance to a second cavern.

"This is where we can bunk down," David said. "It's been used before. There are signs of human habitation. Look! A pile of firewood and matches. Even a kerosene lamp."

He laid out some of the larger logs, then placed smaller kindling on top and struck a match. I waited with bated breath, and the tiny flames licked around the sticks.

"I can understand how fire made such a difference to the life of Stone Age people," I said.

"Let's try and dry out our clothes."

He fashioned some of the larger pieces of wood around the outside edge so we could drape our clothes over them. We couldn't see to the back of the cave, so I lit one of the kerosene lamps and explored. There was a draught which carried the smoke away towards the larger cave so there must be an opening there.

"I wonder if the bushrangers left any of their contraband up here," I suggested, my spirits rising as I saw some charm in our situation.

"It's on the map, and I think there have been more people here recently. I imagine that if there were any looted gold, it would have been found long ago," replied David.

"There is a tunnel here, but it's small. I would have to bend down to get along it," I said.

"If it caved in, then we would be in a right fix," replied David. "Come back, and we can set up for the night."

I returned to the fire, rolled out my swag and spread David's blankets. Then, I removed my jacket and sweater and hung them on the logs. I climbed into the swag, wriggled out of my wet jods and handed them to David, who hung them up. I didn't even let myself think about snakes, but I explored every inch of the inside of the swag with my legs to check that there were no creatures in it with me. I peeled off my muddy socks and draped them over my boots, roasting near the edge of the outer flames. I shook out my hair and combed it with my fingers. I couldn't be bothered to search for my hairbrush. Every inch of me was sodden and frozen, and I hoped I wasn't going to catch pneumonia.

David discovered the bacon sandwiches we had packed when we left.

"They're a bit old and stale," he said. "But I'll toast them by the fire; they're better than nothing. I've got some flour, salt and water, and I can make up some damper to cook in the fire when it burns down to embers."

Never had stale toasted sandwiches tasted so good.

"What is that?" I asked as David fiddled with a square tin and iron bars that made a tripod.

"It's a camp oven made out of a biscuit tin; you hang it over the fire, and you can cook the damper inside it, rather than the dough getting all sooty in the embers. You can bake cakes as well."

"If we had the ingredients."

"Here are some Arnott's arrowroot biscuits, an Australian treat," he said, handing me three oval-shaped biscuits. And a mug of sugared tea."

The fire was warm. My swag was cosy, and I had some food in my tummy.

"You know, I've been thinking," I said. "I don't want to rubbish the great poet Banjo Patterson, but if it was a colt by Old Regret that had gotten away, how could he have joined the bush horses without the stallion chasing him off?"

David was silent, considering what I had said. "You're right. It hadn't even occurred to me. But when you read *The Silver Brumby* and understand the social hierarchy of a herd, you will find that a stallion will hardly accept a colt into its midst. The colts are chased away when old enough to be a threat. But remember that other poem by 'Surcingle', in that ballad it was a mare that had joined the brumbies."

"The chestnut mare might indeed join the brumbies, as a stallion would accept a mare but not a colt," I said.

"The description of them chasing and herding the brumbies is brilliant, though," said David.

"Very stirring and heroic, but I don't fancy it myself, and I'm not sure that Sinbad would be up for it," I went on.

"Yes, but in the books, the stallions often leave their herds and go away on solitary expeditions. Searching for other mares, finding out where other stallions are. That might be our best chance. To wait for the stallion to leave the mares and then creep in and hopefully be able to catch the chestnut mare. She might still have some of her bridle hanging on, something to catch her with," said David.

"We still have to actually find them," I said, thinking that there was Buckley's chance of us finding the mare, let alone catching her.

"There is the stallion mound of manure," said David. "That's a sign that there are horses around."

I woke early in the first grey light of picaninny dawn that glimmered through the entrance to our small cave. The horses were restless, hungry and thirsty. I climbed out of the swag and thrust my legs into my jods, which were nearly dry. I pulled on my jumper and pushed my feet into my socks and boots and walked stiff-legged out to the entrance to the larger cave. There was no sign of clouds or rain. The sun rose over the distant mountains, shards of light sparkling on the grass, glinting mischievously.

"It's a perfect day!" I said, utterly amazed.

"It's time for us to do some serious scouting around now. But first, I will catch some fish for our supper tonight.

"How good are you at catching fish?" I asked skeptically.

"Wait and see," he said with a secret smile.

"Do the fish talk to you as well as the horses?" I asked a trifle sarcastically.

He didn't reply. Hunger was making me bad-tempered.

We boiled the inevitable billy of tea with sugar, but no milk and David produced the tin of arrowroot biscuits. They were crunchy and delicious, so I couldn't complain.

I led the horses out and found some grass, as they had had no supper the previous evening. I was content to sit on a log and close my eyes, my face tilting towards the morning sun. The last few days had been exhausting. I would have to toughen up to survive in these mountains. I tried to determine how many days had passed since John had driven me to Corryong. I had lost count. I imagined that the Heywards would be at the Tamworth Show by now. I felt like I had stepped through a keyhole into another world where schedules, days, and weeks didn't matter.

David came back from the stream with a gunny sack that looked full.

"We'll have fish for lunch and supper tonight," he said, grinning and pleased.

I led the horses back to the cave, packed the gear, saddled up, and attached the various implements to our saddles.

"I think we might take the tripod and camp oven as well," said David. "They could be useful if we're up here for a while. Hopefully, we can find some sign of human habitation, and they can give us more flour, tea, sugar and meat or vegetables if we're fortunate."

"Will we manage if we don't find anything?" I asked.

"Yes, we'll be fine. I'll shoot some rabbits, and we can roast them in the oven," he said.

"I think that rabbit is better stewed than roasted," I replied. "The meat is rather dry."

"We don't have a pot," said David. "Next, you'll want us to carry a kitchen sink."

"You're the one who wants to take the oven and tripod," I retorted.

We set off across the face of the slope, heading down towards the smooth, upward-tilting plains broken up by rocks and stunted timber below us.

"If I were a stallion, I would bring my mares down here to graze," said David.

We rode for several hours. The rain had washed away any tracks. Then, I spotted another huge pile of manure.

"Look!" I shouted.

David went over to look at the mound.

"You know some of this is fresh," he said. "I think that they must be around here somewhere."

We rode on searching for tracks, and at dusk, I heard a sound in the distance. A high-pitched whinny.

"Did you hear that too?" I asked.

"Yes," replied David. "I think we're getting closer. Do you want to keep going for a few hours? The closer we get, the better."

We risked not setting up a camp in daylight, but the excitement of finding the horses was too much for us. The weather was mild, and we could sleep out in the open as long as we could find a clearing to light a fire.

"I'm looking forward to grilled fish," I said.

When all the light had faded, we found a clearing. There was a stream nearby, and I led the horses down to drink, then we tied them to trees on long ropes so that they could move around and crop the grass. David had built a fire, and using the tripod, he cooked the fish in the oven.

"I found some sweet potatoes in the bottom of the saddle bag. I've sliced them up so they cook quickly."

"That's good. I'm so hungry I need some carbohydrates," I said, remembering our domestic science lessons at school on different food groups.

We sat in the dark listening after our meal, which had been delicious if a bit meagre. The bush sounds were all around us, but then we heard the ringing sound of hoofs on rocks above us, higher up on a nearby hill.

"You know the stallion might have smelt us and come to check us out," said David. Our horses were restless.

"At least we're not riding mares that he might want to steal," I said.

I found it hard to sleep that night. I kept half an eye open in case the stallion came storming into our camp and attacked us, pounding and stamping us with his enormous hoofs, screaming with fury that we were encroaching on his territory.

When I woke, I was still in one piece. There had been no murderous attack. David was up. The fire had been stoked up, and the billy was hanging from the tripod. He had gone down and led the horses to a fresh grazing place. Magpies were carolling cheerfully from the high branches of a gum tree.

I poured myself a mugful of tea from the billy with a generous shake of sugar, stirring it with a eucalyptus twig. I ferreted through the saddle bag and found the biscuits. I did like these arrowroot biscuits. I imagined that they would be even better with a generous slathering of butter.

David walked back and warmed his hands at the fire. I poured him a mugful of tea. When we drank all the tea, we were ready to go. I saw a small, cuddly creature delicately stepping across a branch in the tree watching us intently.

"Look up there! What is that?" I asked.

"It's a possum."

"So cute!"

"I think it has a sharp, snooting, snouting sort of face," remarked David.

We set off, our eyes glued to the ground, searching for tracks. After riding for three hours, slowly winding across the hillsides and descending towards the plains, we found a few hoofprints pressed into the soft ground. On we rode. We were momentarily distracted by two substantial flightless birds, like ostriches, but called emus. Their faces were fierce but rather silly. They fluffed their feathers at us and stalked off.

"They've got tiny brains," said David. Then we were watching for tracks again. I noticed some fresh droppings, which I pointed out. Excitement was crawling up into my throat.

"Let's stop for some lunch," said David.

"No, no, let's keep going," I replied.

"This is not going to be over today. Even when we find them, we'll have to work out a way to get the mare. We need to pace ourselves."

We built a fire, boiled the billy, and put some fish in the oven.

"Look over there, climbing up that tree!" exclaimed David in a whisper.

I couldn't see anything. He got out his rifle, carefully aimed and fired. Then I saw it. A big grey goanna fell to the ground with a thump. I had never seen such a creature, like an ugly, grey, scaly little dragon with a long yellow stripe on the underside of its tail.

"What are we going to do with that?" I asked doubtfully.

"Eat it," said David, starting to carve up the animal.

"Does it taste good?" I asked.

"Well, I wouldn't say that. It's a bit like a cross between muddy fish and tough chicken. But it will be a good meal or two for us."

"Delicious!" I said in hollow tones.

"I'll just roast up some slices. We can keep it in the saddlebags and have it as snacks," said David, ignoring my skepticism.

While it was roasting, he carved up the rest of the meat and wrapped it carefully in some brown paper to bake it that night.

I ate my fish, which was delicious, and then tentatively chewed a piece of the goanna meat. He was right; it certainly wasn't tasty.

"Could we shoot one of those cows we see sometimes?" I asked.

"Well, they're branded, meaning they belong to someone else. I mean, if we were starving, it would be justified. But with such a large beast, the butchering would be a big task with my one knife, and then we'd have to carry it around for days. But it is an idea if we're up here for weeks."

"Weeks!" I squeaked.

"Hunting brumbies is not one day's entertainment."

My thoughts went to the Heywards and Cappie, who was probably being jumped by one of the others. I hoped that they didn't mind me absconding in the way I had. I felt like I had entered another universe where time wasn't recorded in the same dimension. One day was blurring into another as we ate around a campfire, slept and rode through the bush: no newspapers, radio programmes, schedules or appointments to keep.

"Look over there! In the trees! There's a horse skulking," said David.

"You're right. It's a horse. It's watching us! Do you think it's the stallion, and he will come storming in and attack us?"

"I don't know. Just sit still, and we'll see what happens. I'll inch over towards the horses and get hold of their reins. We don't want them to gallop off. It would be a long old walk back to the Old Mill."

The horses were looking towards the bushes where the strange horse was lurking. Their ears pricked; they were on alert. We waited with bated breath. Eventually, it stepped out into the open and looked at us with what I imagined was a pleading expression.

"It's a gelding," said David. "It's certainly no angry stallion."

"You're right," I said. He was a poor specimen of an animal. He wasn't healthy and thriving. "Look, his mane had been trimmed where the

headpiece of a bridle goes over the top of his head. I think he was a domesticated horse and has been running in the bush."

"I don't imagine a stallion would welcome a random gelding joining the band. Perhaps he's been hanging around the edges of the herd," said David.

"He seems to want to be with us," I commented as the brown gelding walked tentatively towards us. "He's been lonely, rejected and wandering in the bush."

"He's not been doing well. He's no bush horse," said David.

"We have to rescue him. I'm going to catch him. I wonder what he's like to ride. We could maybe ride him and let Old Joe have a bit of a rest. If we had a pack saddle, he could carry some of our gear."

"Steady on," chuckled David quietly. "We don't even know if he's rideable."

"If they were trimming his mane like that, he was ridden," I replied.

I took a shorter piece of green hide rope and approached the gelding quietly. He looked at me with trusting brown eyes. I approached his shoulder and slipped the rope up around his neck. He stood quietly. Then I stroked him, and he leaned into me. I fashioned a halter around his head.

"We can lead him with us," I said.

"He probably would follow along with no rope," said David.

"I think you're right."

We set off shortly afterwards. Our number had now increased to three horses. David led the new horse.

"What shall we call him?" I asked.

"I think Fred," replied David.

"I suppose that's as good a name as any," I replied doubtfully.

The wild horses' tracks were easy to follow as we descended towards the plains, and the ground became softer. The path was less stony. I was worried about how we might catch the chestnut mare. It all seemed like such a glorious adventure when we set out. But even when we found the horses, it wouldn't be easy to spirit her away from an angry and possessive stallion.

As dusk fell, we saw them, finally. We were high on a ridge, and there was a valley below us. Perhaps about thirty horses who were settling for the night grazing. The light was too dim to make out the chestnut mare. We couldn't even be sure that we had found her. She might be running with any of the other herds in the mountains.

We made camp and sat around the fire. The cheerful flames flickered and burned. There were a few more fish, and then it would be goanna. I decided that perhaps I wasn't destined to be a hardy bush person. I longed for a warm, soft bed and one of the breakfasts served at Blainstock Castle when we had paying guests, with chafing dishes on the sideboard loaded with kedgeree, bacon, and home-grown eggs in various forms. I knew that I was torturing myself by thinking of this food, and then I was longing for a bowl of rich, creamy custard poured over spotted dick.

I tossed and turned half the night and then slept late. When I woke, the three horses were grazing quietly, but David was gone. I wriggled out of the swag and poured myself a mug of tea from the billy hanging above the fire. It tasted acrid as we had used up our sugar supply. There was a goanna tail for breakfast, but I couldn't face it. Wistfully, I remembered the sumptuous hampers Mrs Heyward had prepared for us at the shows. I didn't dare contemplate the delicious breakfasts of kedgeree, scrambled eggs, mushrooms, toast and jam served at the castle.

"This sucks," I muttered to myself. I rummaged through the saddle bag and found one crumbly arrowroot biscuit, which was my measly breakfast.

I looked up when David walked back into the camp.

"She's there, the chestnut mare. She's in the herd," he said excitedly. "She's got the remnants of her bridle wrapped around her head, but the saddle's gone."

"That's good to make sure it's her," I said doubtfully. "But how on earth are we going to get her? We can't just walk up to her and lead her off."

"I've got an idea."

I was so gloomy that I didn't even ask him what his big idea was. It was strange but now we had actually found her it seemed like a huge anti-climax. I was sick to the back teeth with the whole thing. I didn't care about the reward or the glory of catching the mare and returning triumphant. I just wanted to go home.

"One packet of flour is left in the other saddle bag. Why don't you stay in camp this morning and make some damper? I put a wood pile there, and you can bake it in the oven. I'm going back with a rope, and I'm going to stalk the herd. You can move the horses around to fresh grazing, take them down to the stream and rest up a bit," said David, divining my black mood.

I didn't argue with him. I just sat there staring into the dwindling flames. It was all I could do not to suggest that we give up and find the quickest way home, and then I could go back on the showjumping trail with the Heywards.

He slipped away with a rope, and I stayed in camp. The sun was shining brightly, entirely at odds with my black mood. I took the horses down to the stream and tied them in a new place with fresh grass. It would be good for them to have some time off. I got my hairbrush out of the saddle bag and tried to untangle Fred's mane. He rubbed his head against me affectionately. I wanted to talk myself into a better mood. At least, if nothing else, we had saved him from a miserable fate wandering through the bush by himself. I wondered how he had ended up here. I checked him all over. He had no scars, and if I screwed up my eyes and looked at him from a distance, I saw that he would be a good-looking horse if he were in better condition. I wondered what he might be like to ride. He stood at about 15.3 hh, a nondescript brown. His head was fine, his ears small and pointed, his eyes kind. He looked like a thoroughbred. I thought that perhaps ninety per cent of riding horses in Australia were ex-racehorses.

I mixed up a damper and put it in the oven after I had built up the fire. Then, bored with my own company, I walked down to the edge of the ridge to see if I could make out what David was doing. If the herd had moved off and he was following on foot, I would be stuck here by myself. The thought was terrifying. I was entirely reliant on this man to get me back to civilisation. I liked him. He was kind, patient and a good conversationalist, but I didn't feel any particular connection with him. In my head, I knew he was my father, but that element of affinity was very vague. I guess I just wasn't brought up to have a father. Perhaps Mummy was right, and I would never find myself a husband either. That was not a promising prospect!

Disconsolately, I looked down at the plain below. In the full light of day, I could see the stallion was apart from the herd, snatching mouthfuls of grass, looking warily about while he chewed. He was a good-looking horse, tall, well-set, powerful, a deep brown colour. He wasn't happy, and I wondered whether he had smelt David, who was undoubtedly lurking somewhere down below with a greenhide rope, hoping that he might be able to catch the chestnut mare.

I searched the bush around the herd's edge, looking for any sign of David. He wore drab browns and greens and would blend effortlessly into the scraggy bush. I couldn't see him.

The stallion was increasingly nervous weaving around erratically sniffing the air. I hated to think what he might do if he found a man nearby. He began to round up the mares driving them into a tight bunch. He was squealing and nipping their rumps. I imagined that soon I would hear the thunder of their hoofs as they set off at full gallop away from us. It might take us days of riding to catch up with them again. I was despairing. There would be no heroic gallop chasing them, like in the Banjo Patterson poem. I wasn't going to be plunging down any sheer cliffs on my weedy thoroughbred which I have to admit was not something that I would relish.

As I watched, the stallion trotted in a wide circle around the mares. His head was low, tail flowing, his hoofs elevated with every step. Once they were bunched together, he drove the herd into a small valley almost directly below the ridge from where I was watching. The valley was bounded by two steep rocky slopes. The mares milled around nervously in this naturally enclosed area. They sniffed the air, tossed their wild manes and whinnied anxiously. In the confusion of the restless horses the young foals lost their mothers and rushed around screeching in their high voices, adding to the general chaos. I spotted the chestnut mare. She was on the edge of the crowd, obviously still an outsider who the other mares treated with suspicion. She was certainly a good-looking horse, worth the reward and the determined pursuit of so many men trying to recapture her.

Then the brown stallion left his mares and galloped back onto the plain. He lifted his head high, sniffed the wind, trumpeted and screamed, then rearing up he pawed the air. He seemed to be challenging someone or something. I hoped this violent reaction was not against David who might have his stock whip but hadn't taken his gun which was in its leather sheaf attached to the stock saddle in the pile of tack close to where we had slept.

I waited. I could sense that something was about to happen. Then I saw movement on the other side of the plain. A lone horse was galloping towards the brown stallion who was standing stock still staring at the oncoming animal. Then I realised it was another stallion. The two of them were going to fight. The challenger was a beautiful golden chestnut with a flowing flaxen mane and tail. He was heavier with solid muscled shoulders and rump. If I were a betting person, which of course I wasn't, I would have put my money on the chestnut. The brown stallion snorted with fury.

I watched fascinated. There was a preliminary dance where each animal reared, pawed the ground, ears flattened, eyes narrowed and flashing as they circled each other. I had never seen anything like this. To me horses were sacred creatures, loving and obliging if sometimes mischievous or ill-mannered. This was a serious conflict. I had heard that stallions often fought to the death. The brown stallion snaked his head, ears flattened, teeth bared, he aimed a savage bite at the chestnut's neck and then he swung around on his haunches, double barrelled him in the ribs, and then turning back reared up and attempted to strike with his forelegs. The chestnut twisted and received only a glancing blow on the shoulder. The double-barrelled kick missed its target altogether.

They drew apart and faced each other. Then both leapt at the same time, up on their hindlegs they crashed and became interlocked, each seeking to bite the other's neck. They staggered back and again faced each other. The brown stallion was lighter, thus more nimble, than the thickset chestnut. They danced around each other for several minutes.

Out of the corner of my eye I saw a flash of chestnut. I turned my head and was astonished at the sight of David riding the mare bareback up the rocky slope of the little valley below me. Of course! How fortuitous that the brown stallion's attention was distracted from his mares and David was stealing Diplock's horse.

I looked back at the stallions, suddenly afraid that the brown stallion might see his new prized mare being ridden away by a hated man. But they were oblivious of nothing but each other. They were snaking their necks, their teeth bared. The brown managed to get a grip on the chestnut's neck just above the wither. For a moment he hung on and then the chestnut managed to fling himself away. At this rate they could be fighting for a long time. Although one fatal blow and it might be all over.

I looked back and saw that David had made it to the top of the gully and was disappearing over the slope. He would ride her back here. Then it dawned on me. We were going to have to decamp and get away as quickly as we could. Otherwise, if the brown stallion won the fight, he would be tracking the mare and he would come to reclaim her.

I sprang into action. I packed up our gear and led the horses in to saddle up. Then I noticed that Old Joe was limping. His offside foreleg was slightly swollen. This was a disaster. We couldn't leave him behind or he would probably be killed by one of the stallions and he could hardly fend for himself in the harsh mountains. If David rode the chestnut mare, then we could lead him. He would slow us down but there was nothing else for it. I stuffed our belongings into the saddle bags and attached them to the saddles. I dowsed the fire and rolled up the swag with David's blankets and tied them behind the saddle on Sinbad.

By the time David rode into camp on the mare we were nearly ready to go.

"Good thinking, Jill. We've got to make tracks," he cried, as he slid off the tall chestnut's back.

I was about to reply when we heard a trumpet-like scream from down on the plain.

"I hope they're still fighting and that's not the brown stallion realising that one of his mares has gone."

"I know. But listen, Old Joe is lame. You're going to have to ride Diplock's mare."

I threw the saddle on the mare, not waiting for him to agree, slipped a bridle on her adjusting the buckles and we set off.

"Will we follow our track back the way we came?" I asked.

"No, I think if we go down the hills, beyond that plain there is a road that leads back to the Old Mill. It's the way they brought the timber out. We should be safer on the road. The wild horses usually avoid it and use their own tracks through the bush."

I hoped that he had read the map correctly. I had no idea which way we should be going. We rode back in the direction we had come but this time plunged down several gullies so that we were on lower ground. I wondered what was happening with the stallions. Hopefully the fight would go on for a long time and the brown stallion, if he won, would be too tired to immediately follow us. We had the gun but the thought of actually shooting the stallion if he came for us was horrendous. It would be better if we just cracked the stock whips to frighten him off, but better still if we got well clear.

With two horses being lead, one slightly lame, we were travelling more slowly. I know that this might have been of lesser importance, but I was conscious of the fact that we had nothing for dinner tonight except for a few unappetising remnants of goanna. There was no time to stop and fish. It might be possible to shoot a wallaby or a rabbit. I didn't mind killing rabbits, but the wallabies were so sweet, and I was conscious that this was their homeland, and we were the interlopers.

We came to a stream, and I remembered something I had read.

"If we walk down the stream then we won't leave tracks or scent."

"Yes, you're right. We're having to make it up as we go along," said David ruefully. "The cold water might help the swelling in poor Old Joe's leg. I'm feeling guilty having to tow him along like this."

We found a place where we could walk into the stream and made our way down the hill. The horses slipped and slid a little and we had to watch out for rocks, but it wasn't too bad. We kept going for thirty minutes and then the stream was rushing steeply down the hill. It was too hard to keep going as the current was much stronger and the bed of the stream too rocky. We climbed up the bank and found a narrow path that wound between scrubby teatree bushes.

By now it was late afternoon, oblique shadows slanted through the trees, and I wondered how long we could keep going. Then the track widened and miraculously there was a hut in front of us. The idea of sleeping under a roof and not in the open was too tempting.

"I think we should stop here for the night. The stallion will be much less likely to approach human habitation. Old Joe needs to rest. It's not fair on him," I suggested.

There was a lean-to built on one side of the hut with enough room for all the horses to be tied for the night. It would be more secure than leaving them tethered on the grass. There were still a few hours of daylight so they could graze until nightfall.

"I'm going to try and catch some fish," said David. "Do you want to get the fire going. You could use the last of the flour to make some damper so at least we have something to eat in case the fish aren't biting."

It was a relief to be out of the saddle and moving around. I took the billy down to the stream to fill it with fresh water and went back to light the fire. As usual there was a stock of good firewood that had been stacked inside the hut. I got the fire crackling and producing heat and then hung the oven above it. I kneaded the dough and shaped it into a loaf and put it carefully inside the stove. Then David came in with four fat silver fish.

"Oh delicious!" I said. "They will do very nicely for supper."

"I'll gut them and get them ready to cook if you want to water the horses and then bring them in and tie them in the lean-to. We can have an early night. I wondered if we should take it in turns to keep watch?" said David.

"I suppose we should. It would be tragic to lose the chestnut mare after all this," I replied uncertainly. I had been looking forward to a comfortable night. Our adventure was proving extremely arduous. David offered to do the first watch and I fell immediately into a dreamless sleep, in front of the fire. I didn't wake all night. Then, at dawn I realised that David had sat up near the horses dozing lightly and hadn't woken me for my watch.

"Thank you for letting me sleep," I said gratefully.

"There was no sign of the brown stallion, but I think we should push on as quickly as we can. Here, look at the map. I think we're here, another five miles through the scrub and hopefully we'll hit the road and then it's about twenty miles." I looked at the map and hoped that he had got it right.

"Twenty-five miles seems a lot for one day," I said.

"Let's lead out Old Joe and see if he is still lame," said David. "We'll go as far as he is able today."

The old thoroughbred was barely uneven in his gait.

"He's much better," I said with relief.

We ate the last of the damper, saddled up and got going. The five miles through the scrub was hard going. We had to go in single file and the spreading wattle branches brushed us as we passed. The ground was soft in laces and then there was scree, like a covering of rocks that slipped and gave way beneath the horses' hoofs.

Finally, we made it to the road which was a huge relief.

"Seems like your reckoning on the map was correct," I said.

"I wasn't sure," laughed David, "but I acted confident to reassure you."

"Now it's a mere twenty miles up this dirt road and we're there. Hopefully we'll make it by dusk," I said.

No brown stallion had come storming down on top of us and we became more confident that he wouldn't be pursuing us. I was hoping he hadn't died, nor the beautiful golden stallion. Perhaps they had both been exhausted and the chestnut had slunk away back to his own herd

Chapter Fourteen – The Rescued Horse

We got back to the Old Mill by late afternoon. Three men were sitting around the burning campfire in the yard. They turned to stare at us as we arrived. I was riding Sinbad and leading Fred, the rescued gelding. David was riding the chestnut mare and leading Joe.

"*You* got her!" exclaimed the old man, nursing an enamel mug.

The emphasis was on the word 'you'. We were the last of the hunting pack to be expected to have won the prize.

"'ow is she?" asked the other man.

"She's sound," I said.

"Probably in foal," added David.

"You get the 500 smackers," said the third man sourly.

"We better pop 'er in tha truck, get 'er back ta Diplock. 'e'll be right pleased ta see 'er," said the old man.

"We'll come too, and then you can drop us off at Corryong if that's not too much trouble," said David.

"Surely," he assented. "Leave their gear on them," he added as I started to undo the girth.

"We borrowed Sinbad, so I'll leave him here for his owner, with his tack. Can you tell him thank you for lending him to me?"

I found it weird to be transporting horses with their tack on. I still wasn't used to the rough and ready ways of the mountain men. The new horse, Fred stepped confidently onto the truck. I think he was happy to be going back to civilisation.

It wasn't far to the Diplock's station. It was a big spread with an impressive sprawling homestead. Mrs Diplock rushed out when she saw the truck drive up.

"You found her!" she shouted with glee, seeing the chestnut mare's head over the top of the truck's sides. "Rex! Rex! Come here! They've found her."

Mr Diplock hobbled out; his leg was in plaster, and he was struggling on crutches.

"Fan-bloody-tastic!"

We led the mare down the ramp. Her owner ran his hands down her legs and then stood back, leaning on his crutches, and examined her critically.

"Thank you so much," he said. "What's your name, I don't think we've met."

"No, I'm a newcomer, live at Corryong," replied David. "This is my daughter Jill. We went off on our own after a day with the group and managed to track her down."

"Come inside. Let me give you a drink, and the reward of course," said Mr Diplock.

The front door led to a long corridor with rooms off each side. The truck driver came with us.

"Come into the living room," said Mrs Diplock.

"What would you like?" asked her husband.

"Scotch, if you've got it," replied David.

"Me too," added the driver.

"Soft drink, please," I said.

"Here's the reward," said Mr Diplock, handing over a fat envelope.

"Thank you very much. Very much appreciated," replied David.

We left soon after that. We wanted to get home and the two horses off the truck.

It was a relief to get back to the house. David handed the driver a five pound note out of the envelope and thanked him for bringing us back. He accepted gruffly, eyeing the envelope stuffed with money sourly. I didn't care. We were back and the idea of a hot shower was very tempting, but first we settled the horses.

"You take them around the back and I'll just pop in and light the chip heater, so we've got some hot water," he said.

That chip heater was annoying. At home we had a gas boiler that heated the water. Here, it was a black stove that sat in the bathroom and a fire had to be lit to get it to heat the water to be used for bathing. It was a palaver but given enough time the water came out piping hot and it was what I wanted most.

I unsaddled both horses and rubbed them down. Then I prepared them a small feed of crushed oats and lucerne chaff. I didn't want Fred to have too much. He would have to get accustomed to hard feed again. His hoofs needed some attention. His toes were long, and the hoof wall was cracked and chipped. His mane and tail were matted, and it was going to take hours to comb them out. I thought I might wash his tail and apply copious amounts of conditioner before I attempted this task. Imagining him in better condition he could be a quite reasonable looking horse. He was perhaps a better riding prospect than Old Joe for David. He was certainly easy to handle.

"How did you end up in the mountains?" I asked him. "Perhaps you've got an owner who is missing you dreadfully."

I went in and stood under the hot steaming shower for at least five minutes, soaping myself all over, and washing my hair.

"I bet you feel better now," said David, when I emerged wearing clean clothes. "I've ransacked the cupboards and I've got two tins of baked beans. There's some eggs and a side of bacon, no fresh bread. But there is a couple of tins of peaches."

"Sounds utterly sumptuous," I sighed.

"You sit down, and I'll serve you."

"But you haven't showered yet."

"The chip heater'll need another half hour to heat up the next lot of water. Let's eat."

Never had bacon, eggs and baked beans tasted so good. I wolfed it down, then looked around.

"Seconds coming up," said David, piling another helping onto my plate. "Then a tin of fruit each."

"I don't think I ever want to sleep in the bush again," I said. "I'm just a prissy miss from England."

"You coped amazingly well," said David. "Many would have given up and complained and you didn't. Stoic to the last."

His words of praise affected me greatly. It was the first time I had ever had a father telling me how well I had done. I felt hot tears in my eyes. I dashed them away.

"You should have your shower now," I said gruffly. "Then, surely, it's an early night. No poetry recitations. All I want to do is sleep inside four walls with a roof, on cushions."

The next morning, I woke early and stretched luxuriously. I could think of no reason why I had to leap up. No bitter tea without milk. No horses to lead down to the stream. No anxious eye on the weather.

"Do you want breakfast in bed or are you getting up?" called David.

"I'll get up," I said and went out to the outhouse in the back garden.

"I've been into town and got us some fresh bread, straight out of the oven, and some milk, and some sausages, steak and vegetables. I think today we're going to be feasting all day," he said.

"Oh! Wow! You sound like you love food as much as I do!"

"I think so," he said grinning broadly. For the first time I felt a sense of kinship with him. Not father and daughter, or whatever father and daughter might be, but an idea that we were the same blood. I suppose there is nothing like roughing it in the mountains far from civilisation to forge a bond with someone.

"I thought I might try and tidy up Fred a bit," I said.

"Yes, we should try and ride him today, just a bit around the paddock then you can see what you think of him. Also, I've got an idea for the reward money. We could go half each and I want to try and buy an old truck. Then I might be able to pick up a bit of work doing some transportation in the local area. I saw a notice in the store's window this morning that the local garage is selling an International with a crate on it." He was clearly excited about this idea. "It's 11 years old, an International AR-160, 6 tonner, four speed manual, four on the floor, with a two speed Eaton differential. That gives you eight forward gears and two reverses. With the wind behind it downhill it can go up to 60 mph, but its average road speed is 50 mph. Only 200 pounds! The only bad point is that it used to be dark green, and someone painted it yellow. Not a very good paint job."

"Gosh!" I exclaimed, not really understanding a word of this technical description but I did understand the unfortunate colour change. "About the reward I really don't want half," I said. "It was you who caught the mare. I just came along for the adventure. I'm not desperately broke or anything. I don't need it. You should buy yourself a truck and it can set you up with a useful little business."

"Are you sure?" he asked.

"Yes, I'm sure. I really don't want the money at all," I said. "But I would like to have a ride on Fred. See what sort of horse he is. He'd certainly do you better than Old Joe who might deserve to be retired."

"Well, my riding has certain improved. You know riding that chestnut mare bareback up the side of that steep gully was a challenge, but I didn't have time to think about it in the heat of the moment."

We ate our way through a monster breakfast of sausages and tomato sauce, fried tomatoes and fried bread. When I couldn't eat another bite, we went down to see the horses. We gave them a feed and set to work grooming Fred. Then we saddled him up with David's old stock saddle.

"You ride him first," David said. "You're the expert."

"Sure," I replied.

I adjusted the stirrups and mounted. Gently I squeezed with my calves. Fred dropped his head and walked forward. I could feel his hocks coming under him and he mouthed the bit. He was well-schooled! We walked around the small paddock, and I pushed him into a trot. He sprang forward smoothly and trotted beautifully. I pressed him for some collection, and he responded immediately. Then I asked him to lengthen his stride and he was off in a lovely extended pace, like a ballet dancer pointing his toes. I gave him the correct aid for canter leading with his near fore on a straight line and he responded accurately. I asked for a flying change, and he was onto it.

"This horse is so well-schooled!" I exclaimed.

"I've never seen anyone ride like you," said David.

"Loads of people can ride like me," I muttered ungraciously. I didn't really think. Of course, David wasn't involved in the equestrian scene.

"Do you want to try him over a jump? I could cobble something up for you," suggested David.

"Yes, why not? Although jumping in a stock saddle isn't ideal," I said.

I let Fred walk around on a loose rein. He was brilliant but he wasn't in great condition, and I didn't think it was fair to ask too much of him.

David dragged over two 44-gallon drums and put a pole across them.

"Can you find another pole to give him a ground line?" I asked.

All he could come up with was a short pole, but it was enough for Fred to be able to judge the height of the jump. I circled him at a canter, and he approached the jump confidently. He increased his pace slightly and popped over like a true professional.

"Can you make it higher?" I asked. "I think we've got one brilliant horse here."

David found two kerosene tins and put them on top of the 44-gallon drums, making the jump about four feet high. Again, Fred jumped it as if it were nothing.

"I think that's enough for now," I said. I dismounted and loosened his girth.

David was looking thoughtful.

"Do you think we should try and find his real owner?" he asked.

"Yes, you're right. Perhaps the Heywards might know of someone who lost their showjumper?"

"We've got to get you back on your showjumping tour," he said. "By my calculations I've got to drive you to Bourke as they would have left Tamworth by now. I'm going down to the garage to look at the yellow truck this afternoon. If it all pans out, we could drive it up country. You know it's about a thousand miles."

"That's a long way," I commented.

"Australia is a big wide country. I need to get used to its ways," said David with a smile using his recently-learned Australian accent.

"Are you thinking what I'm thinking?" I asked.

"I suspect that I am. We'll take Fred with us. You can have an extra horse to jump, and someone might recognise him."

"Same as what I was thinking!" I said.

Everything worked out perfectly. The truck was 'bonza' as David described it. He bought it that very afternoon, filled it with petrol and we planned to leave the next morning.

Chapter Fifteen – Driving North

David spread another map on the table that evening and showed me the route we would take.

I read out the names of some of the towns struggling over the unfamiliar sounds of the words, "Little Billabong, Wagga Wagga, Coolamon, Kamarah, Barellan, Binya, Erigolia, Rankin Springs, Cargelligo, Naradhan, Lake Cargillian, Murrin Bridge, Euabalong, Eubabalong West, Mount Hope, Gilginnia, Cobar."

"It's going to be brilliant. Give the little truck a run, and I can see more of this huge country. I've heard that Bourke is a big show," commented David. "Every man and his dog will be there. It's a good chance to see the landscape out west."

"I'll see much more of Australia," I said. "First the hoi poloi of Sydney, then Manly and the bohemian elements, Bowral, Dunslains, the Snowy Mountains and now I can see what's out west. I read somewhere that the north wind is like a dragon's breath, which withers trees and starts bushfires. Weatherboard houses stand on stumps to keep them safe from the white ants. Imagine insects that can destroy your house!"

"I've asked Ted, my neighbour, to keep an eye on Old Joe and feed him every day. Now, let's get a good night's sleep, and we'll set off on yet another adventure. I can't think of a better travelling companion than my daughter," said David fondly.

I felt embarrassed and a little overcome by this praise, so I merely grunted ungraciously and turned away.

We set off early. Fred was happily standing in the truck, his nose above the sideboard, sniffing the air and looking around with interest. We went north back through the mountain country. I made sure to take a good look. I wouldn't return to this neck of the woods on this trip.

I would like to give you a detailed account of our journey, like a travelogue, but truth to tell, I think our mountain adventure took it out of me, and I slept for a good part of the way. In the evening, we parked by the side of the road and led Fred around, let him graze and then put him back in the truck but untied. The crate could carry eight horses, so it was about the size of a loose box, and we put straw on the floor. I had increased Fred's hard feed rations, and he had a haynet tied to the side of the truck for him to pick at while we travelled.

David slept outside in the swag every night, and I bunked down on the bench seat in the front of the truck in a nest of pillows and blankets. We had the tripod, the camp oven, and this time a frying pan. We bought fresh milk, bread, and butter at stops along the way, so our camping trip was luxurious compared to what we had endured in the mountains. We had supplies of sausages, bacon and eggs, so there was no need to kill animals to eat.

The journey took us four days, and I wondered if the show might be over by the time we got there and if we would have to drive back to the Heywards' place in Sydney. As we went west, the landscape radically differed from the country in the southern tablelands of NSW or the Snowy Mountains. As we got closer to our destination, I saw vast paddocks of cotton plants.

We got to Bourke, which sat on a bend in the Darling River. As we drove through the town, I saw many Aboriginals who were the original inhabitants of Australia. I stared in amazement at them. I don't think I had ever been to a place where there were dark-skinned people.

"They call this town the gateway to the outback," said David. "The expression 'the back of Bourke' means anywhere that is very remote."

"I thought we'd been in the outback for miles already," I replied, overcome by the vastness of Australia.

"Henry Lawson wrote that if you know Bourke, then you know Australia," said David. "Also, when I researched, they said this was home to many Afghan camel traders who traipsed huge distances in the outback."

I was reassured that the signs pointing to the show were still up and that it was the first day of this two-day event.

We drove into the showground.

"You know I've never been to an Australian show before," said David excitedly, like a kid.

We trundled around towards where the horse trucks were parked. On the way, we passed a merry-go-round, a pieman calling out his wares, a stockman sitting on an orange crate playing a ukulele, a boxing tent, and the yards set up for the rodeo. A billycan race was in progress. You had to ride bareback carrying a billycan of water, jumping half a dozen low obstacles.

"Look! Look! It's the Cannon twins," I shouted, recognising one of them dashing over the finish line with their billy can.

I knew the Cannon twins were from Sydney, but my time there was limited, and I wasn't sure of their address. Now, here they were!

David stopped the truck, and I jumped out and dashed up to the one who had just finished the race. She remembered me instantly and greeted me with great enthusiasm.

"Jill Crewe, I should have known you would tip up in the most unlikely of places, all the way out here at Bourke Show!" she said. The other twin came up, hugged me, and slapped me on the back.

"I'm here to meet with the Heyward family," I said. "Do you know them? Robbie, John and Norah?"

"The Heywards …, " said Norrie. "Yes, I think I've heard of them but haven't met them."

"We found a gelding in the Snowy Mountains. He was wandering around utterly lost and rejected by the brumbies, so I brought him up here. We thought we might find someone who knows who his owner is. He seems like a good jumper."

"That is random!" exclaimed Dorrie. "Even for you, Jill. I suppose you were riding around the mountains and happened upon this horse."

"Well, of course not!" I exclaimed. "We were up there helping in the hunt for a valuable mare who had thrown her rider and run away with the wild bush horses!"

The twins were roaring with laughter at this point.

"Oh, help! I'm being called next in the billycan race. Look! We've got a spare horse. Why don't you enter Jill?" said Dorrie. Without waiting for an answer, she went over, put my name on the list, and handed over the entry fee.

I dashed back to the truck, where David waited patiently, not wanting to intrude.

"I've been entered in the billycan race," I said.

"Is that the Heywards?" he asked.

"No, it's the Cannon twins. I met them in England a few years ago. Do you mind driving around, parking up and unloading Fred? After this, I'll find you, and we can locate the Heywards and get set up."

"Anything you like," he said agreeably, smiling at me.

"Who is that man in the truck?" asked Dorrie.

"It's my father. He lives in Australia," I replied without thinking, completely forgetting the need for secrecy.

She didn't comment. She hadn't known that my father was supposedly dead when we had hung around in England, so there was no need for any more improbable explanations.

I borrowed a hard hat to go in the billycan race. I have to admit that I didn't cover myself with glory. I actually fell off over the second jump and got soaked with water. Everyone laughed uproariously. Then Robbie walked up, he had been watching the race and asked me where I had suddenly appeared from and how I got a ride on one of the famous Cannon twins' horses. I could see that explanations would become the order of the day.

Now that I had spilt the beans to the twins about my father being here, I knew I would have to come clean to Robbie and Norah. Keeping secrets just wasn't my forte. I comforted myself with the thought that Bourke was a long way from anywhere.

"I have to go and find David, unload Fred, and say hello to your mother," I said to Robbie.

"I'll take you to the camp. What's this horse, Fred?"

"We found him wandering in the mountains, and I've ridden him a bit. He seems well-schooled, and I thought I might enter him in a competition if he goes well over the practice jumps."

"So, you found some random horse in the wilderness, and you're going to try and jump him," said Robbie quizzically.

"Yes," I replied shortly. "After all, people find amazing horses pulling carts through city streets and all sorts of places. Why not wandering through the mountains?"

Robbie shrugged, and we set off to the area where the trucks were parked. I found David waiting in the old yellow truck along the way, and he drove behind us. There was room to park beside the Heywards' vehicle, and the introductions began. Mrs Heyward, aware of the story of finding my father, exercised her considerable social skills, and it all went smoothly until Robbie began asking some searching questions, and John jumped on him and squashed him. To distract attention from all this, I unloaded Fred, and the Heywards looked him over critically.

"He needs shoes," said John. "There is a farrier here. I'll ask him to come over and fix his feet up.'

"He does look a bit raggedy," said Norah. "I think he needs some tender loving care."

"Imagine how you would look if you'd been wandering through the mountains, chased by stallions!" I retorted, suddenly feeling very protective of my latest equine charge.

"Why don't we put a jumping saddle on him and try him over some practice jumps," John suggested.

"I've got a feeling he's been a jumper in a previous life. He might get recognised by someone, and we can reunite him with his owner," I said.

I declared this bravely because I knew it was the right thing to do, but I secretly fancied Fred for myself. Not that I could ship him back to England, so there was no future for the two of us together.

"We don't have any spare stables booked," said Mrs Heyward

"He'll be right tied to the side of the truck," I said, thinking how we had spent the night with the horses in the lean-to up in the mountains. "Let's give him a few hours to rest before I ride him. It's been a long trip up here."

Mrs Heyward pressed food upon us, and I was so grateful to be fed more decent tucker. I still have bad memories of that goanna. It would take me weeks to get over the bush camping experience.

"I am amazed that you should be such great friends with illustrious people as the Cannons.

We have seen them around some of the shows over the years, but none of us have ever struck up an acquaintanceship," commented Norah.

"I met them in England," I explained.

"Tell us what adventures you had in the mountains," said John. Everyone was clamouring for information.

Then the Cannons turned up and were invited to join our meal. The focus of attention switched to them. All the Heywards were anxious to get to know them, and I was let off the hook trying to explain everything.

"How do you know Jill?" asked Norrie.

The Heywards happily described their trip to Blainstock Castle in Scotland.

"I suppose you two have not been sitting around letting the grass grow," I said to the twins.

"No, indeed," said Norrie. "Dorrie is now engaged, would you believe it? She's getting married in Sydney next week. Jill, you must come. You can be the guest of honour, especially as you taught us to ride!" They laughed merrily, and Robbie, John, and Norah's eyes widened like saucers at this revelation.

"Tell us who you're going to marry," I asked. "I suppose he's a showjumper."

"Not at all," said Dorrie. "He's a very bookish Associate Professor at university with good prospects for becoming a Professor within a few years. He teaches history and writes very serious stories about the First World War. Isn't that marvellous!"

"Fantastic!" I said, wondering how on earth that was going to work. "You know Ann is engaged too. She's marrying a vet called Henry. He is a jolly good egg, and they've been together forever."

"And you, Jill? Are you being courted?"

"No," I said shortly. This was a sensitive subject. Then, the conversation turned to events at this show. The showjumping events were scheduled for the following day.

"Are you competing in the Table A?" asked Norrie.

"Yes, we're all entered, and Jill will be on Cappie. I don't suppose we have much hope against you two," said Robbie.

"As you know, anything can happen in showjumping," said Dorrie.

"Now that your new horse has been rested, let's look at him over the practice jump," said John to me.

"Oh yes! Let's!" exclaimed Norah. "What do you call him?"

"We decided on Fred," I replied.

I tacked up with Cappie's bridle and saddle and led him around.

"I've arranged for the farrier to come and do him at five o'clock today," said John.

"Thank you," I said. Then I mounted and walked him around. The others followed me over to the area where there was a practice jump. I trotted and cantered for at least twenty minutes. I wished that they would all go away. I felt nervous being the focus of attention. Finally, I had no excuse to put it off any further. The jump was about four feet, and I cantered towards it. He jumped it so easily and casually that you would have thought it was a cavalletti.

Everyone clapped, and I felt even more embarrassed.

"I'll put it up," said Norrie. She raised it another foot, and again, we sailed over it easily.

"Try him in a few small circles and ride at an angle. See how responsive and supple he is," suggested Dorrie.

I did as she instructed, and he was very good at turning and tight circles.

"You should take him in the Table A tomorrow," said Robbie. "He's easily as good as Cappie."

"I suppose I should," I replied. "Have you ever seen him before, any of you?"

"No," they each answered.

"We can put the word out," said Norrie, "and see if anyone has lost a showjumper. Bring him over, and let's look at his teeth."

They examined his mouth.

"I think he looks about nine years old," said Dorrie.

"Perhaps only eight," said Norrie.

"And no distinguishing marks," added Robbie. "You might have scored yourself an excellent horse, Jill."

"Well, he's no use to me. After this show, we're all heading back to Sydney. So, which of you wants a showjumper?" I asked.

"Let's see how he goes tomorrow," said John.

No one was clamouring for him, but tomorrow would be the test. If he went well, I did not doubt I would be having to decide who should have him.

"Do any of you want to have a go on him?" I asked.

"I will," said Norrie.

She mounted, and he circled and jumped just as competently as when I had been riding him.

"He's a good horse," declared Norrie, "indeed it might be worth buying him. How much do you want, Jill?"

This floored me. I wasn't even sure I was entitled to sell a horse I had found. What if his real owner recognised him and wanted him back?

"I have no idea. Let's just see how he goes tomorrow."

David had mainly sat quietly on the edge of our group, but at one point I saw that he and Mrs Heyward had been having some serious, quiet discussions. He moved over and sat beside me.

"They're good people, the Heywards," he said. "The twins are a lively pair."

"Yes, they've been good to me. We met them when they came to stay at the castle."

"I know, Elinor told me. Do you think you should sell Fred?" he asked.

"I don't know. What do you think?"

I heard myself asking my father for advice. Somehow, I was slipping into a father-daughter relationship, which felt very strange.

Chapter Sixteen – Jumping Fred

"They're calling the first competitors," said John. "Come on, you've got to put Cappie over the practice jump a few times, Jill. We've put you down early in the running order, so you can warm up Fred before he jumps later."

"Of course," I said. Cappie felt just the same as usual when I rode him around the practice area.

The course was a decent size. The jumps sturdy, the cups deep enough not to let the rails fall easily but the distances between some of the jumps were tricky. The third jump was a very high five feet six with no wings. On landing there was a sharp turn to the left and five long strides, or six short strides to a treble, three elements, with two strides between the first and second and then just one stride between the second and third. Then another sharp turn and only three strides to a very wide triple. That was three strides with the need to accelerate to get over the triple. I didn't imagine that there would be too many clear rounds. I was feeling quite confident on Cappie now that we had grown accustomed to each other.

John was back on Hussy who had got over her temperamental stage. As usual, Robbie was on Pepperpot and Norah on Annie. The Cannon twins were riding matching greys. They were quite sturdy looking horses, Andalusians crossed with thoroughbreds and apparently, they used them for trick jumping as well. They had developed a famous act where they jumped without bridles and just ropes around their necks. I thought perhaps Cappie might be a third in such a performance.

I rode into the ring. Cappie shook his head vigorously, testing the bridle, but the extended throat latch was firmly in place and his trick didn't work. We jumped the first and second, quite straightforward ordinary jumps then I attempted a little collection before the gate as there was such a sharp turn on landing. I turned my head to the left and we pivoted as we hit the ground, and I kept a tight rein so that we counted six strides before the treble. We were over the first element, two strides and the second but Cappie slightly stumbled on landing and although he made a brave attempt, he didn't recover in time for the third element, and we crashed through. I decided that we should retire, there was no point in continuing and I was worried that he had banged his forelegs quite hard on the rails.

"Bad luck, Jill!" called the Cannons as we left the ring. Mrs Heyward took Cappie from me and we swapped the saddle and bridle over to Fred.

"I'll take Cappie back to the truck," she said. "You go and warm up Fred."

I rode Fred away. I did want to watch the twins and see how they went. I heard Norrie's number being called and the loudspeaker was telling everyone how famous the Cannon twins were. I walked Fred over to the edge of the ring so that I could watch. She galloped into the ring with a flourish. She was wearing a made-to-measure riding jacket, black with silver buttons and piping around the collar. She looked very dashing. Her horse was bucketing around. I didn't quite approve of this showing off. It was obvious that she was stirring him up unnecessarily, but she was such a gifted rider she would get away with it. It was a beautiful silver-grey gelding, 16 hh with a black mane and tail, which I suspected was dyed. She had a European-made very forward cut jumping saddle and a fancy bit that I didn't recognise. When Ann and I had known them, they had been superstars but since then my riding had jumped up several levels, but I realised that I would never have the flash and dash of the twins. But that didn't mean I couldn't compete against them and hope that sensible good riding might carry the day.

She went clear, and so did Dorrie. It would have been an anti-climax, if they hadn't. I noticed that Dorrie's style was not as flamboyant as Norrie's. She was fast but she seemed to jump with more precision. Robbie and John also went clear, Norah had four faults. I was determined to go clear on Fred. I felt that I had something to prove.

Unlike Cappie, he responded to my usual style of riding, I collected him, using my legs and executing a number of half-halts. We cantered into the ring, I bowed to the judges and the bell rang. It helped that I had jumped the course before. We sailed over the first and second jumps, then the gate and a sharp turn, over the treble, one, two, and three. This time we finished the course, and we went clear, and I could hear the burst of clapping and the shouts of congratulation from the Heywards and the Cannons.

"This is going to be a good jump-off!" said Robbie. From our group there was Robbie, John and me, and the two Cannons. There were also five others. I was determined to try my very best.

The air was thick with tension. I think we were all determined to go clear and the fastest. The shortened course consisted of the very high fence, now at five feet nine with no wings, that was jumping away from the collecting ring, then six strides on to a plank fence, only five feet but with no ground line, which was very difficult, and then you either cantered in a wide circle around the treble which was not to be jumped, alternatively you could land from the plank fence and turn sharply for the next jump which was an ordinary straightforward fence, one more jump along that line and a sharp turn right over a hogsback and through the finish. I wasn't sure whether to take the wide curve around to the third fence or to cut across and jump with perhaps only a stride before take-off. Even before this decision had to be made, we had to get over the plank fence with no ground line.

Norrie was the first to jump. She bucketed in with her flashy style, which I assumed was the only way she ever rode. In this case she didn't pull it off. Her horse misjudged the second jump with no ground line, and they crashed through. This seemed to shake her and although she had surely planned to cut across the quick way she wavered for a moment and then took the long way around. She cleared every other jump, but her time was slow.

Then it was Dorrie. I wondered if she would be more careful. She cantered in, her mouth set in a grim determined line. I guess if one twin didn't win then it was up to the other. Dorrie galloped through the start, over the first, a slight check and then she very deliberately placed her horse for take-off over the plank fence. She was turning to the left even before they landed and without a moment's hesitation they were over the next two jumps and then a turn on the haunches to the right and they were flying over the hogsback and through the finish. It was an awe-inspiring round, and their time was very fast.

"Looks like the rest of us are jumping off for second," said Robbie. He was right. I didn't imagine that anyone would be able to beat her time.

Robbie rode in next, and he was obviously going to go for broke. Pepperpot was dancing on his toes, wound up tightly. They galloped over the first narrow jump and then without pause he went straight for the plank fence. I held my breath, but they cleared it and then he spun around and over the next fence and the one after, but then they had to turn right for the hogsback and he misjudged it and they came up short and Pepperpot hit it. That was four faults, although his time was considerably faster than Norrie's. So, at that moment he was standing second out of three competitors but anyone with even a slow clear would beat him.

I think John had decided that would be his strategy. He cantered in a very controlled way, over the narrow jump and then slowly towards the plank fence. He cleared it and they cantered strongly but in a wide arc so they could approach the third jump with a perfectly place take-off, over the next and then a sharp right. He kept Hussy bouncing up and down like a ball, riding her at a very collected pace and they were over the last jump and only then did he lean forward and race towards the finish. Their time was not brilliant, but they were clear.

"Well done!" I shouted as he rode out of the ring.

I was the last to jump, so I rode away and didn't watch the five other riders in the jump-off. The tension was too great, and I wanted to be calm so that I could do my very best when my turn came. Three went clear with reasonable times, one faster than John, two others slower. The other two had eight faults each going too fast and taking too many risks. That meant that Dorrie was first, another rider second, and John third.

I had to make a decision. I was riding a horse that I had never competed on before. A horse that had been running wild in the bush for a number of months, who had only had shoes put on him the evening before after months barefoot in the mountains. The obvious course would be to be sensible, ride carefully and try to improve on John's time. I decided not to be sensible. I would take all the chances and ride to win, even against the famous Dorrie Cannon.

I would have to cut the corner to the third fence to be in with a chance and I would have to ride fast at the difficult plank fence trusting that Fred could judge the height. I galloped through the start straight as an arrow over the narrow fence and then the plank fence. Fred took it perfectly and we sailed over with just the right amount of clearance, then landed and spun to the left. There was only one stride and over the third fence, and I pushed Fred on a little faster for the fourth fence and then a sharp turn to the right, over the hogsback and we galloped through the finish as if we were winning the Grand National.

I knew that we were clear, and I waited to hear the time. It was just one second slower than Norrie. I didn't care, as far as I was concerned it was perfect. We were second but it was a glorious achievement. I loved Fred. He was perfect and I wondered whether it would be possible to fly him back to England. My placing had bumped John down to fourth, but he didn't mind. He was a good sport and slapped me on the back and congratulated me.

They award ribbons, rather than rosettes in Australia. This one was special, and I would treasure it.

"We definitely want to buy that horse off you," said Dorrie.

"But what if his real owner comes forward to claim him?" I asked.

"We'll take that chance," said Norrie.

"I have no idea what sort of price I should ask? Let me think about it," I said.

Norrie didn't look happy, but she acquiesced.

After we had been presented with our ribbons I rode back to the truck. I had been worried about Cappie and I got out the ice, put it in the bucket and started to sponge down his front legs. There was no swelling and perhaps I was being over-careful but I had a bad feeling.

"Perhaps you're getting a big old for this game," I said to him quietly. He looked at me wisely. I didn't want to say anything to the Heywards. He was their horse and any such decision to retire him would be up to them.

We sat down to lunch, and no-one mentioned the Cannons' offer to buy Fred. David and I walked off when we had finished eating.

"I have no idea what to do," I told him. "I don't think I've got the right to take money for Fred. I don't feel like I really own him."

"I can see why you feel like that."

Then it came to me.

"I shall give him to John Heyward," I said.

"Oh," said David noncommittally.

"He was very kind driving me to Corryong." I didn't add that he stayed the night in the hotel just in case I wasn't comfortable staying at my father's place. "Norah doesn't really care about showjumping, and Robbie treats it all as a joke. I think that John deserves a really good horse. That Hussy is too unreliable."

"Well done!" said David. "I think you've made the right decision."

"Now, it is just the timing," I said.

I decided that I wouldn't jump Fred again today. He wasn't fit and he had done so well it would be best to finish on a good note. The others were doing a Six Bar competition this afternoon. They assumed I would ride Cappie but I bowed out.

David and I went over to the ring side to watch. There were six fences in a row with two strides between each jump, each one higher than the last. It was a little like the high jump in that if you cleared the fence then you were in the next round. In this case, you were given two chances to clear the jumps, and then they were raised, and all remaining competitors would jump again.

I knew that John especially liked this type of competition. I hoped that Hussy was in one of her good moods today.

The Cannon twins jumped first. They were fiercely competitive, and this included against each other. Norrie would be desperate to do well after her failure this morning. Time was not an issue. It was solely a matter of clearing each jump. However, it was necessary to go reasonably fast, the two strides between each jump were long, allowing for the horses to gallop to gain momentum to clear the final jump.

Norrie galloped in but she was exerting a measure of control and concentrating properly, not just showing off. The beautiful silver horse flowed over the jumps, leaping higher and higher and clearing each of them. The crowd clapped and cheered, and she waved to them as they galloped back to the other horses and riders.

Dorrie was next, riding her identical silver horse she jumped in the same way as her twin, and she also went clear. Again, the crowd cheered and clapped.

Two other competitors went, each knocked the final jump, had another go and again knocked one of the jumps. Robbie came in waving to the crowd, as always the clown. Pepperpot was fast and nimble, but he didn't have the power of some of the bigger horses to jump impossible heights. They went clear but I could see that the little roan was straining, I didn't think he would get round too many times as they started to raise the heights.

Then Billie Tennant galloped in on a fresh horse, a magnificent bay stallion with a long mane and tail. It was whispered that it was of brumby stock. Its mother had been shot by brumby hunters and Billie had bought a job lot of youngstock, and this horse had been one of them.

"I've been thinking about the brumbies," said David. "I know I'm still a raw beginner when it comes to horses, but I would like to learn to break them in. There are all those brumbies running wild. I wouldn't want to shoot them, of course, but perhaps some of the colts and fillies could be brought in and domesticated."

"Now you've got your truck it would be useful. Are there any sales where you can buy brumby youngstock? In Devon they have a muster of Dartmoor ponies every year and then sell them at auction. It's the same with New Forest ponies. Perhaps there is something similar here?" I suggested.

"I don't know. I'll have to look into it. I like the idea of spending my days with horses, training them," said David.

I almost said, 'you're a chip off the old block', which was a little back-to-front, but if he really did have the ability to communicate with horses, and he was certainly patient, then I could see him succeeding in this venture.

"If you visit again, then you could show me some techniques for breaking in," he said lightly.

"Sure," I replied noncommittally. I guess with me leaving for Sydney tomorrow with the Heywards he would be heading back to Corryong on his own. The issue of us seeing each other again had not been mentioned before.

Billie Tennant jumped wonderfully, went clear at his first go, and we clapped politely.

"Between the Cannons and Billie, the Heywards are up against some stiff competition," I commented, changing the subject.

John galloped in on Hussy. He was riding in his usual no-nonsense style with technical skill. They jumped smoothly down the jumps and just tipped the last obstacle. Without any fuss, he turned and cantered circles until they put the poles up and this time, they jumped clear. David and I clapped loudly and shouted our congratulations.

Norah had decided that Annie had enough with the Table A that morning and she didn't attempt it. Soon everyone had done the first round and there were fifteen competitors for the second. Again, the Cannon twins went clear, as did Billie Tennant, five other competitors and John. Pepperpot was overstretched and didn't make the final height, even with two attempts.

So that made nine competitors for the third round. The heights now looked astronomical. I was musing over how Balius, my gelding back in Scotland, might manage over such jumps. I thought with his enormous scope he would do very well. Perhaps I should set up such a course at Blainstock when I got back.

The Cannons were again clear and so was Billie Tenant. Four of the five other competitors were out and then it was John. I was crossing my fingers, my arms and my legs for him. I did wish that he might succeed in this competition. I held my breath as he went down the line and he was clear. Hussy really did jump well when she had a mind to. I made a mental note never to have a mare for competitions, although to be fair, my own little Copperplate who was now regularly ridden by riding school students was faithful and true and didn't engage in female histrionics like Hussy.

There were now only five combinations left and the poles went up again. The tension along the ring side was palpable. It felt like all the audience were holding their breath. Dorrie galloped in but she was going so fast that her horse flattened and for this type of height one needed parabolic jumps, so she knocked two rails. She was to go again and this time she slowed down, but still she hit a jump, so she was out. Next was Norrie, who also hit a jump, but in her second attempt she went clear. Billie Tennant's horse just couldn't make the height of the last jump, not even with another attempt and he was out. The other competitor was also out, so John had everything to play for.

If he went clear, then he and Norrie would be the only two contenders so he would be sure of at least a second place.

Norrie went first and she was clear, then John did as well. The heights were now reaching to the sky. Over the loudspeaker there was an announcement that this was the 'battle of the giants' and people were hurrying over to the ring side to watch. The local photographer was positioned in a way to get a dramatic photo for the regional newspapers.

Norrie was cantering slow circles, sitting deep in the saddle she was letting her horse stretch down before she gathered him together. They jumped the first, two strides, the second clear, two strides, the third clear but he pecked on landing and didn't recover sufficiently for the fourth jump. This must have disheartened him, and he veered away from the fifth jump. They would have to try again. Somehow her horse just didn't recover his nerve. He refused the first jump and she nearly tipped off as he swerved. It was all up to John, if only he could go clear then he would be the winner.

Again, I crossed all my body parts and held my breath. I so hoped that he would succeed. He cantered in and Hussy looked tiny next to the huge jumps. John appeared not to be fazed. He cantered to the first jump, and they were clear, the second clear, the third clear, the fourth clear, the fifth clear and if only he was clear over the final one then he would have the victory. Hussy suddenly looked daunted, but John urged her on with uncustomary vigour and she rose to the occasion, soared into the air, tucked up her hoofs and landed. There was a storm of applause from the crowd and John smiled broadly. I was jumping up and down with excitement and shouting my head off.

As John rode out, we all gathered in the collecting ring to congratulate him, even the Cannons who might be extremely competitive but were also good sports. Norrie was second, and Dorrie and Billie Tennant were equal third. They were all called in for the presentation and John was presented with a fancy sash, an envelope of winnings and a rather bizarre china vase that would look entirely out of place in their modern Sydney house. I hoped he wouldn't drop it during his victory round. He tucked it awkwardly under his arm. Norrie and Dorrie's horses tried to overtake him, but they valiantly held them back so as not to steal the limelight.

That evening we had a small party. Mrs Heyward had gone into town and bought some fizzy white wine with plastic glasses. We all toasted John's success, then Fred and me, and the Cannons, then the toasts got silly, and we thought up all sorts of improbable things to which we could raise our glasses.

On the morrow I would say good-bye to my father and who knew when we would see each other again. Our reunion had been successful. We had certainly got to know each other and I was glad, because I had dreaded it so much.

Chapter Seventeen – Falling Out of Love

We returned to Sydney and the horses seemed very happy to be back in their Centennial Park stables. The place was abuzz with the latest news. Just across the park was the inner-city suburb of Surry Hills where an infamous underworld figure had just died at the age of 84. Of course, I had never heard of her. It was Kate Leigh, who in her heyday, from the 1920s until the 1940s, had been a crime lord. She had been an unmarried mother and ruled one of the infamous razor gangs that waged their murderous warfare in Sydney streets, terrorising honest citizens as they engaged in internecine conflicts. They slashed faces with razor blades when it became too dangerous to carry guns. She had ruled the underworld as a purveyor of sly grog, which is illegal alcohol, a brothel keeper, cocaine dealer and fence for stolen goods. What I found rather strange is that she seemed to have been well-loved and well thought of not only by the criminal classes but also law-abiding members from the lowest to the highest. She was famed for her warm heart.

"They say that she was a *good friend* of our grandad, that is Dad's father," boasted Robbie mischievously.

No one seemed perturbed by this announcement. It was merely a part of their family history.

"If he were still alive, I'm sure he would have attended her funeral."

"So, she was well-respected for being a crime queen?" I asked hesitantly.

"It's our convict heritage," said John stiffly. "There's a strong streak of rebellious anti-establishment in our makeup."

I was tempted to ask if we could go to the funeral. Perhaps it would have been disrespectful to attend a funeral of celebrity who I hadn't actually known. But it promised to be a spectacle that would go down in Australian history.

No sooner had we got home than Norah was persuading me to go out with her so she could rush over to visit Michael.

"What will his crowd think of Kate Leigh?" I asked, still mystified about the way Australian society functioned.

"I don't really know," she admitted. "But when we meet up, I'm sure they'll be talking about it, and you can find out. I suppose it's like a sociological object lesson for you."

"Perhaps,"I replied doubtfully. "Sociology wasn't a subject studied at my school." In fact, I didn't really know what sociology was.

Mrs Heyward gave us permission to 'go to the beach'. She did so with a pained expression. Of course, she knew exactly what Norah was planning to do. We caught a bus to Circular Quay and then the ferry over to Manly. I was still thinking about the death of Kate Leigh. Norah was trembling in anticipation at seeing Michael. She had been away for weeks, and she was desperate to be reunited with her lover.

We arrived at the café where the gang usually spent the afternoon and Michael was there. He greeted us warmly. His eyes were glazed, and he did look as if he had taken drugs. But this was not the worst of it. He was seated at the end of the table, right next to an exotic looking woman wearing a diaphanous gown and a feathered turban. She was called Zuleika. She usually lived in Melbourne but Michael and his gang had been down there visiting and she had returned to Sydney with them. She claimed to be a Romanian gypsy who had come to Australia after the war and was famous for her art and bohemian lifestyle. There were stories flying around the table of wild orgies of Bacchanalian proportions. Zuleika was well known as a siren who bewitched men.

Then they began to talk about Zuleika's occult activities. Known for her psychic ability, she had recently held a séance. A rather chubby man with wild dark hair and squinty eyes described how they had all sat around a table draped in dark silk. Dozens of candles and sticks of incense in Eastern holders were placed around the room. There had been an incantation. Things hadn't gone according to the regular order of calling up the dead and it had all become a writhing mass of orgiastic bodies.

Michael made no attempt to pretend that he hadn't taken part in these activities. I stole a glance at Norah, and she was open-mouthed, obviously shocked to the core. I realised then that she was way out of her depth. For all her attempts to join in the arty scene she was really an upper-middle class girl who had attended a fee-paying school who had been seduced by the glamour of a poetic young man who paid no attention to any moral principles of fidelity and exclusive relationships.

"I think we should go," she whispered to me. I jumped up with alacrity and with only cursory farewells we were out of there and back in the fresh air. If Norah was out of her depth, then so was I. I had no idea how to deal with this situation.

Norah was walking blindly down the street, I followed her, half a step behind. We got to the ferry.

"I can't go home yet," said Norah helplessly. "Let's go and have a drink in the city."

"Alright," I agreed hesitantly. "But I would like something to eat as well."

I had enough common sense to know that drinking without eating was not going to be a good idea. We went into a small Italian restaurant and Norah ordered a bottle of house red and I asked for two bowls of pasta with tomato sauce. The wine came immediately, and the pasta took a while and by the time it was plonked in front of us Norah had drunk three-quarters of the bottle and was glassy eyed and ranting.

"Astral spirits! Destiny! Transcendence! Mad sprites are filling my head," she cried in anguish.

I tried to encourage her to eat the pasta, but she was wild with misery and continued to babble. She called for another bottle, and I began to despair. If I took her home like this it was going to be difficult to explain. I looked around, searching for someone to help and my eyes alighted on a poster on the wall. It was advertising a play that was currently being staged at a small theatre starring none other than Beau Carlisle who was one of my good friends with whom I had shared many adventures.

"Oh, my goodness!" I exclaimed. Norah was too far gone to hear me. She was in the middle of an account of her despair which she believed surpassed the misery of any woman who had ever been scorned.

I saw that the performance began at 8 pm. In just one hour. I paid the bill and asked the waiter the location of the theatre which was just around the corner. I literally dragged Norah out of there and pulled her behind me to the door of the theatre. There was a small group of people in the foyer waiting for the play to begin. I bought two tickets and then managed to get to the bar and order two cups of coffee.

"A friend of mine, Beau is starring in the play," I explained to Norah.

She looked at me nonplussed.

"What is the play?" she asked, her words slurred.

"Something in Italian," I admitted.

"We don't speak Italian," she replied.

"No, I'm sure the play is in English, Please, please, Norah, this is important to me, please don't make a scene. Here, drink your coffee! When it's finished, we can go backstage and I'll introduce you to Beau Carlisle. He's a dreamboat," I added.

As readers of my previous books will know Beau's film star looks were not a factor in our friendship. He had always been caught up in disastrous relationships with older married women. But Norah wasn't to know this. I hoped I might distract her from her disappointment with Michael by introducing her to a gorgeous young man.

Then the curtain went up and there was a stage set in Italy with a *trattoria*, red-checked tablecloths, and a deep blue Mediterranean Sea painted on the backdrop. Mungo, which was my nickname for Beau, appeared on stage in all his handsomeness, bright blue eyes and smooth blonde hair. He was the hero and a swarthy looking, flashing black eyed man was the villain. Inevitably there was a woman they were fighting over, a very curvaceous red head with a pronounced Australian accent. She was an unlikely casting for an Italian maiden, but I guess you have to use your imagination when it comes to drama.

I looked sideways at Norah who was now slumped in her seat, her eyes half-shut. She wasn't paying much attention but at least she couldn't drink here. The play's storyline was predictable but entertaining and I oohed and aahed enthusiastically with the small audience. The theatre was only half-full, and I felt that I needed to contribute vociferously to cheer on the actors. I did vaguely wonder how Beau had descended from starring in quite big films to this small production in the Antipodes but thought perhaps he had found himself in a tight spot again with a husband of an older woman and had decided that discretion was the better part of valor.

The interval was short, and everyone crowded back into the small foyer where a bar was set up. Norah acquiesced when I insisted that we drink coffee and I bought a bag of crisps, which strangely they call chips in Australia.

Then we trooped back into the theatre, took our seats and watched the dramatic, if predictable, conclusion to the play. As soon as the curtain went down for the final time, I dragged Norah towards the backstage entrance. It wasn't even a matter of talking our way in. The production was modest and there was no huge crowd struggling to get to meet the stars.

We found Beau in a small cupboard-like dressing room. He was wiping the greasepaint off his face in front of a mirror that was lit around with flashbulbs.

"Mungo!" I called.

He turned quickly, probably wondering who on earth knew him by this name, but his suspicious expression vanished in a trice when he saw it was me.

"Jill, darling!" he said and getting up flung his arms around me melodramatically. "Fancy meeting you here so many, many miles over the sea and far from home."

"I'm here on holidays," was the shortest explanation. "Let me introduce Norah Heyward. I am staying with her family in Sydney."

"How do you do," said Beau flashing his most seductive smile and putting out his hand.

Nora was visibly impressed, and I think for a moment she had entirely forgotten her overwhelming distress over Michael's perfidy.

"We're all going out for drinks and some supper. Would you like to join us?" asked Beau.

"Oh, yes please," I replied. This was just the distraction that Norah needed. But I would have to make sure she didn't drink another bottle of wine.

Strangely I found myself the centre of attention when we ate at the same Italian restaurant that Norah and I had visited earlier in the evening. I entertained everyone with an amusing account of my adventures in the Snowy Mountains and the hardships I had survived. The tale of eating goanna elicited grimaces and groans. I saw that Norah had slid in beside Beau and she was fluttering and smiling at him. He certainly did his part responding enthusiastically. Perhaps he had got over his penchant for older women and now found younger ones more to his taste.

By the time our supper was finished Norah was visibly drooping.

"Time for us to go home," I announced.

"I'll come out and find you a cab," said Beau gallantly.

"I would like you to come to our place for dinner," said Norah. "I know Mummy would adore to meet you. Do you have any nights free?"

"We're not playing on Tuesday and Wednesday evenings," said Beau.

"Here's our address. Come on Tuesday night. In fact, if you come in the afternoon we can play a game of tennis," said Norah.

I smiled quietly. I don't suppose Michael or any of his friends had been invited to tennis and dinner at the house in Rushcutters Bay. Norah nodded off in the cab and I managed to drag her upstairs. John was prowling around waiting for us and helped me get her to her bedroom. I told him what had happened with Michael. He looked angry.

"I'm glad she's rid of that loathsome little creep," he declared stoutly. "I know that Mum and Dad will be pleased. I only hope this actor chap isn't just as bad."

I hoped so too. It would be extremely unfortunate if I had lured Norah into a bonfire of disappointment after she had jumped out of the frying pan. I would have to have a word with Beau that he was to be on his best behaviour.

Chapter Eighteen – Dorrie's Wedding

Dorrie's wedding was being held on the day before I was scheduled to fly home. Norah and I had been pondering my outfit for some days. My young Australian friend had unkindly dismissed any of my own dresses and I had to admit that she was right. Apparently, it was a grand affair, and I had invited Beau to be my partner. Being seen with an international film star, I thought, was important that I wore something that was both stylish and appropriate to the occasion.

Norah forced me to sit down in the kitchen and concentrate. She flicked through the pages of countless fashion magazines and talked to me about outfits and whether I thought they would suit me. Then she dragged me around innumerable dress shops. I had no idea that Australians were such avid buyers of fashion, but then I had not really plumbed the heights of Australian upper-class society. After flicking through countless racks of dresses, I was in despair. Nothing appealed to Norah. So, she took me to visit Mrs Heyward's dressmaker and asked for her opinion. I had to stand on a dais in the middle of her work room wearing a simple plain shift and she circled me like a vulture with narrowed eyes as if she were planning where to attack me and from what angle. I felt extremely uncomfortable during this exercise.

Obviously black, white or red were out of the question for a wedding and green was considered unlucky. She instructed her underlings to drape me with various fabrics so that she could discern the colour that would best suit my fair complexion, blonde hair and perhaps rather unremarkable blue eyes. Eventually, she pronounced that a hazy floral design that had the look of impressionism with a mixture of blue, yellow and grey might be best. A dress that fell just below my knees which would show to advantage my shapely calves that had been honed by so many years of riding, with a flouncy skirt, a narrow waist and billowing sleeves. I was struck dumb with horror at this plan and what was even worse was that I might be photographed and appear as a footnote in the social pages.

I submitted silently and let the dressmaker, named Madame Sylvestre, and Norah decide upon everything. She promised to have the dress ready for the first fitting in just two days. Then I was dragged to various shoe shops with a swatch of the material so that we could purchase the correct shoes. Mrs Heyward volunteered to lend me a very discreet necklace that sparkled with real diamonds and matching earrings. I attended the first fitting and three of the young dressmaker assistants fussed around, nipping and tucking here and there, then deciding on the exact length of the hemline.

We picked up the dress with a final fitting on Friday and then I had to submit to a visit to Mrs Heyward's Double Bay hairstylist who was to do something with my unruly locks that had grown into a fuzzy mat after my time in the mountains living like a wild person.

Beau was instructed to match his tie to the fabric of my dress, and he assured Norah and Mrs Heyward that he would borrow something appropriate from the theatre wardrobe. He promised not to apply greasepaint to his handsome face, and we were set fair for our appearance at the wedding.

The day dawned bright and sunny which was hardly unusual for Sydney and the service was to be held at St Andrews, a Church of England cathedral. The reception was at a very grand hotel within walking distance, the Observatory Hotel. Dorrie was to arrive at the venue in a fancy carriage pulled by four white horses. It was decorated in gilt and resembled something that the British royal family might use.

The Cathedral was a Gothic design and quite an amazing piece of architecture. There was a grand façade with heavily ornamented towers and tiny pinnacles. It was very British in design. The best of English tradition.

There were several hundred guests and we whirled into the melee. My dress which I had thought would be utterly gruesome was in fact very light and floaty and did make me feel like a minor princess being escorted by a handsome prince. We received many admiring glances and there were whispers murmuring around us, 'Is that Beau Carlisle?' and 'Who is he with? I don't recognise her!' I was happy to be a mysterious unknown woman and we found ourselves adopted by a gang of showjumpers who had frocked up for the event.

Dorrie did look divine, and her handsome academic brushed up well. There was a large wedding party with five bridesmaids all in pale pink and five bookish-looking best men. I was interested to see Norrie and Dorrie's parents who were a handsome couple, well-known amongst upper-class circles in Melbourne society. The groom was from more humble origins and his parents looked careworn, ordinary and uncomfortable.

Dorrie had seated us at the showjumpers' table at the reception and the food was extremely delicious. There was seafood and veal medallions and crispy salads, and I munched my way through several platefuls.

There were endless toasts and we watched Dorrie and her new-husband dancing. Then, we all danced the night away. I think it was the grandest wedding I had ever attended.

The next morning, I was ready to leave, my bags packed. I had brought presents for my family. For Hamish I had chosen a Dinky toy tip truck. It was made of cast alloy, red with a blue tipper body. For Mummy a pair of sheepskin boots to wear as slippers during the winter at the castle. For Richard a book on bushrangers and for Ann an Akubra hat. For Dinah Dean a copy of the magazine Oz which I was determined to read on the plane to give myself an insight into this strange new world that was peeping over the horizon downunder.

I had thought of getting something for Frank but in the end, I couldn't think what to buy him. This was the first tiny hint that I really didn't know him that well. Was he merely a cardboard cut-out to put into the scheme of my dreams for my life? He did tick all the boxes for a boyfriend, but perhaps I just focused on him because he was convenient.

All the Heywards drove me to the airport to see me off.

"What about that horse, Fred?" asked Mrs Heyward.

I looked aghast. I had completely forgotten.

"I want to give him to John," I replied.

"Really!" he exclaimed.

"Yes, you've been so kind to me. I think you are the best person to take him on. And if his real owner turns up, I know that you will hand him over."

"Yes, I will," he said. "Thank you so much Jill, it is a wonderful gesture."

"Yes, indeed," said Mrs Heyward, beaming with approval. "What a good decision."

I walked across the tarmac towards the plane. There was a heat haze in the distance, and I felt overcome. My visit had been so full of excitement, adventures, new friends, not to mention a long-lost father.

THE END

www.ingramcontent.com/pod-product-compliance
Lightning Source LLC
Chambersburg PA
CBHW070937250626
47159CB00009B/3285